CITY FARM

Sammi and Dusty

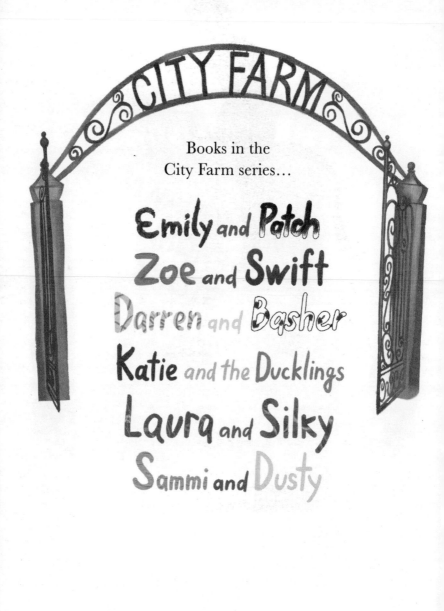

CITY FARM

Books in the
City Farm series…

Emily and Patch
Zoe and Swift
Darren and Basher
Katie and the Ducklings
Laura and Silky
Sammi and Dusty

Sammi and Dusty

Jessie Williams

Special thanks to
Gill Harvey

First published in 2013 by Curious Fox,
an imprint of Capstone Global Library Limited,
7 Pilgrim Street, London, EC4V 6LB
Registered company number: 6695582

www.curious-fox.com

Text © Hothouse Fiction Ltd 2013

Series created by Hothouse Fiction
www.hothousefiction.com

The author's moral rights are hereby asserted.

Illustrations by Dewi@kja-artists

ISBN 978 1 78202 025 7

1 3 5 7 9 10 8 6 4 2

A CIP catalogue for this book is available from the British Library.

Typeset in Baskerville by Hothouse Fiction

Printed and bound by CPI Group (UK) Ltd, Croydon, CR0 4YY

MIX
Paper from
responsible sources
FSC® C020471

To Ibrahima.

Prologue

Sammi stared hard at Miss Crawley, following her lips as she talked. She was telling the class about the Victorian times in England. It had been easy enough to understand what she was saying, at first. She'd written notes about *Victorian History* on the whiteboard behind her. Sammi quickly worked out that this was an important part of British history, very different from anything that had ever happened in Afghanistan. It was really interesting. There had been a queen, not a king, for the whole time!

But as the lesson continued, he began to struggle. There were so many words he didn't know. One word sounded like 'shimni'. Or maybe it was 'chimni'? It seemed to be something the Victorians had lots of. Something in their big old houses that had to be

 7

cleaned by children. Sammi wracked his brains, trying to work out if he'd ever heard the word before. He didn't think he had. In fact, he *knew* he hadn't.

He looked around at his classmates, wondering if they could offer him some clues. But they were all listening to Miss Crawley, concentrating on what she was saying.

'Sammi.' He heard his name, and jumped.

'Yes, Miss Crawley.' He looked down at his desk, avoiding her gaze. *Please don't ask me a question*, he begged silently.

'I can see you've been listening carefully. Perhaps you'd like to go first.'

Go first? Go first at what? Sammi felt his face growing hot. He stared at Miss Crawley, his tongue stuck to the roof of his mouth. He had no idea what she was talking about.

The class waited. Sammi thought he heard someone giggle behind him. *They're laughing at me*, he thought. *Just because I can't speak English properly yet.* He shrugged and glared at Miss Crawley, hoping she'd choose someone else.

'We're describing the life of a *shimni sweep*, Sammi,' Miss Crawley encouraged him. 'Try to find just one word. Anything at all.'

  8

Sammi stared at the edges of his exercise book, where they were getting a bit curled up and grubby. 'I not know what is *shimni*, miss,' he muttered eventually.

'Ah, of course you don't! I should have realized,' said Miss Crawley. 'Let's help him, shall we, class?'

Sammi felt as though he would die of shame. He was already in a baby class with kids younger than him, now they were all making fun of him – even Miss Crawley! How he wished he was back in Afghanistan. There might be more dangers there, but at least it was where he belonged. Now he was nothing but a refugee in a country he knew nothing about, trying to understand lessons in a language he didn't speak. He'd only just learned the alphabet!

'Georgia, perhaps you could stand up and spell it out,' said Miss Crawley.

Georgia was sitting two desks away. She jumped to her feet. 'That's easy,' she said. 'C – H – I – M – N – E – Y.'

'Thank you, Georgia,' said Miss Crawley. 'Now, who's going to explain to Sammi what a chimney is for?'

This was getting worse and worse. Blindly, Sammi got to his feet.

'Sammi! Where are you going?' asked Miss Crawley. 'Please sit down!'

But he wasn't going to sit down. He wanted to

get out of here. He didn't want to hear any more about Victorians or their houses or their silly *shimnis*, whatever they were. He wanted to leave it all behind and go somewhere, anywhere away from here. He left his desk and began to rush to the door.

'Sammi!'

Sammi blundered onwards. He brushed past the last desk, knocking all its books to the floor.

'Hey!' cried the boy at the desk.

Sammi paused for an instant. He hadn't meant to knock the books. He just wanted to get away. He glanced back at the boy. He had freckles and sandy hair, and right now he was looking very cross. Sammi hunted for the right thing to say to him – what did you say when you wanted to apologize? All the words he'd learned in English swirled around like a swarm of bees in his head. One of them pushed itself to the front of his mind and he blurted it out.

'S … s … stupid!' he muttered.

He knew from the boy's shocked face that he'd got it wrong. Completely wrong. Instead of apologizing he'd insulted him! But it was too late now. He wrenched open the classroom door and fled through it, then banged it shut, hard, behind him.

 10

Chapter One

The minute Asha bounced through the City Farm gates, she sensed that something was wrong. It was only early in the morning, but there was already a row of gleaming cars in the car park, and one of them had *County Council* written on it in bright yellow letters. That could mean only one thing: trouble!

She began to head across the cobbles to the barn, but then she heard voices coming from the garden. She changed direction and tiptoed down towards them. She snuck into the pretty garden with its rows of lush vegetables and tumbling flower beds. There, standing right in the middle of a patch of seedlings, were three stange men and someone she recognized: Derrick Jarvis from the council. *What was he doing here?* Asha thought anxiously.

'Of course, some of these trees would have to be chopped down,' she heard Derrick say.

Trees? Chopped down? Asha couldn't believe her ears.

She heard the farm gates open again and rushed back to the car park to see who was arriving. Another car was driving in, this time old and battered with colourful stickers in the windows. Asha felt a flood of relief – it was Kerry Barker, the co-ordinator of the Harvest Hope project. She ran over as Kerry's car door opened.

'Kerry! Derrick Jarvis is here! I can hear him – he's in the garden with a group of men, talking about chopping down trees! Did you know they were coming?'

Kerry got out of the car. She shook her head, her black braids swinging to and fro, her dark eyes flashing with anger. 'No. He should have made an appointment with me. Well, come on, Asha. We'll soon see what he's talking about.'

Asha followed as Kerry hurried over towards the garden. 'Good morning!' Kerry called in a clear, loud voice.

Two of the men turned round, but Derrick Jarvis ignored her, waving towards the fence with one arm and clutching a sheaf of papers with the other.

 12

Kerry marched on towards them. 'Excuse me, Derrick, I don't believe you made an appointment to come to the farm this morning,' she said. 'Could you please explain what you're doing here? And would you mind not trampling all over our lettuces?'

The other men looked down at their feet, and began to step back onto the pathway, muttering apologies. But Derrick Jarvis didn't look the least bit sorry.

'Ah, Kerry. These are the contractors from Deluxe Homes. I wouldn't worry about your lettuces if I were you – they're going to be replaced by something a lot more valuable before long.'

Asha felt her heart begin to thud painfully in her chest. What did Deluxe Homes have to do with their lovely old farm?

'I beg your pardon?' said Kerry.

'You heard what I said, Kerry. We're cutting your funding. We can't go on supporting a tin-pot project like this. It's sitting on prime building land.'

'A tin-pot—!' Kerry's voice rose in outrage.

'That's right,' Derrick carried on. 'There could be quality homes on this site, not just a few sorry lettuces. I know you don't like to hear it, but that's the truth.' He turned to the contractors. 'I expect you've seen all you need to see for now?'

The men nodded their agreement, and Derrick led them back to their cars, talking loudly all the way. Asha stood next to Kerry, watching them go. She couldn't be quite sure, but she thought that Kerry might be shaking.

Asha tried to find something cheerful to say as she and Kerry made their way to the barn, with its higgledy-piggledy roof and ancient wooden beams. Asha's mind was buzzing with questions, but she waited until Kerry had made herself a strong cup of tea and had flopped down onto the comfy sofa.

'What did Derrick mean, about cutting the funding?' she burst out. 'We're always fundraising and selling goat's cheese and jam, and the café sells so many cakes and sandwiches and everything. He can't take that money away from City Farm, can he?'

Kerry sighed. 'Not directly. But City Farm is on council land, you see. So we have to pay rent to stay here. He's right that this is prime building land, and that makes it very expensive.'

'How? What does that mean?'

'Well, as you know, we're right in the middle of the city. People like to live in the centre so that they're close to all the things it offers – their work, shops and restaurants and cinemas and all those things. That

 14

makes the land very valuable and the rent very high. Without the funding that the council gives us, we wouldn't be able to pay it.'

Asha frowned, thinking it over. 'You mean they give money to us in one way, and then take it away in another?'

'Exactly,' said Kerry.

'And if we can't pay the rent…'

'Someone else will. Those contractors will, and they want to knock everything down and build posh houses instead. Derrick knows exactly what he's doing,' said Kerry. 'If he cuts our funding, City Farm would have to close. And so would the Harvest Hope project.'

Asha gasped. She couldn't quite believe what she was hearing. 'But … he can't do that to us!'

'He can,' said Kerry, her voice full of sadness and anger. 'That's precisely the problem, Asha. He can.'

Still feeling shocked, Asha headed outside. City Farm, closing! It was completely awful. She looked over towards the goat pen, with its pretty white fencing, and down towards the pond, surrounded by lilies and reeds … City Farm had become her second home, and she loved it with her whole heart. Whatever would she do without it? When she'd first left hospital after a long fight with leukaemia, she'd been so weak and thin. But thanks to the Harvest Hope project here on the farm, she'd slowly built up her strength. Whenever she'd felt really bad, there had always been something lovely to take her mind off it – a new batch of tiny chicks hatching out, or the rabbits chasing each other around their run, or Stanley the pony greeting her with a friendly whinny…

She wandered round to the paddocks, her heart heavy. Curly and Lizzie, the Dartmoor sheep, came running as she approached their gate.

'Baaa,' bleated Curly, looking up at Asha with hopeful, greedy eyes.

'Sorry, girls,' said Asha, smiling. It always cheered her up to chat to some of the animals. 'Rory will feed you later – it's not your dinner time yet!'

She carried on to the next paddock, where the horses and donkey were kept. Stanley the black and white pony was really friendly, and he trotted over to her straightaway. Asha loved him and Swift, the old racehorse – but Dusty the donkey was another matter! As soon as he saw her, he raised his head and started braying grumpily. It was always a terrible racket, and with all the big yellow teeth he showed, Asha never liked to get too close to him.

But Stanley's ears were pricked eagerly, so Asha decided to take him up to the yard for his daily groom. It was something that Kerry usually did, but Asha knew that Kerry's day was crammed full of other worries. It would be nice to help her. Besides, it was a big job that would make her forget about everything else, particularly Derrick Jarvis!

She had just brought Stanley in and fetched all the grooming kit when Kerry's head appeared over the stall door.

'Oh, thanks, Asha!' exclaimed Kerry. 'I don't know when I would have found time to do the grooming today. I'm up to my ears in everything. But it's great that you're keeping busy – it's the best way. And I've got some other news to cheer you up too.'

'Oh, good!' exclaimed Asha. 'I think I need it!'

'Fortunately, in spite of Derrick Jarvis, life goes on,' said Kerry. 'We've got someone new coming on the Harvest Hope project. He's arriving tomorrow and he'll be coming every weekend for a few months.'

'Brilliant! Who is it?' enquired Asha.

'His name's Sammi. He's a refugee from the war in Afghanistan. His uncle came first, some time ago, and now Sammi has come to live here too with his mother and little sister.'

'What about his dad?' asked Asha.

'Well … I'm not sure. Reading between the lines, I think he's missing.'

'*Missing?* But how… ?'

'People often go missing during wars, Asha,' said Kerry quietly. 'He might show up somewhere, of course, but then again, he might not. Sammi and the rest of his family have to get used to life here, and Sammi's really struggling. He speaks some English but it's very hard for him to follow everything in class. We don't even have the same alphabet. Can you imagine how hard it would be to learn maths or science if the teacher was talking in a language you didn't completely understand?' Kerry asked. 'As well as working out the answers you'd have to work really hard just to figure out what the question is!'

Asha shook her head. 'When my family speak Hindi I can't keep up. It must be like that all the time for him.'

Kerry started combing Stanley's mane. 'We can't help him learn English any faster – that'll take time – but we're hoping that City Farm will help him feel a bit more at home in the UK.'

'He'll love it here, I know he will!' Asha exclaimed. 'There's nowhere as welcoming as City Farm.'

Kerry smiled. 'That's a lovely thing to say, Asha. Let's make sure we keep it that way – while we still can.'

Chapter Two

Sammi gazed up at the big metal sign outside the gates. He pointed out the words to his six-year-old sister Giti.

'It says C – I – T – Y. City. F – A – R – M. Farm,' he read for her.

Giti nodded, taking it all in.

'I don't know why they say you have a problem at school,' commented his mum, in Pashtun. 'You seem to be able to read everything.'

Sammi shook his head. It just wasn't that simple. 'I can chat to people, a bit,' he told her. 'And I can read some things, but I get lost all the time when I'm in class.'

'If you say so,' she said, sighing. 'Well, come on. Let's go in and see what this farm thing is all about.'

  20

Sammi took a deep breath. He wasn't sure what *this farm thing* would be about, either. He couldn't see how it was going to help him. It wouldn't give him the things he missed, would it? Not his friends, his way of life, all the things he'd grown up with – or his dad. And he had no idea why everyone thought it might help him with school. What did a farm have to do with learning English or having to sit in a baby class?

He pushed the metal gates open and stepped into the farmyard. At once, it was as though the bustle of the city outside faded away. He heard a sheep bleating somewhere, and ducks quacking. Then a hen and her chicks made their way across the yard, pecking at this and that.

'Chickens,' said Giti proudly, in English. She grinned up at him. She was learning English so fast it was amazing – and she'd only just started school. Sammi envied her. Soon she'd have completely forgotten the time when she spoke only Pashtun. She'd be way ahead of him!

It was even harder for his mum. Sitting at home, with only his uncle for company every now and then, she was struggling to pick up any English at all. He glanced across at her tense face as a lively black woman emerged from the big building ahead of them, and came over.

'Hello, hello!' said the black woman with a friendly smile. 'I'm Kerry Barker, the Harvest Hope project co-ordinator. You're Sammi, aren't you? And this is your mum?'

Sammi nodded. 'And Giti. My sister.'

'Welcome to City Farm,' said Kerry. 'I expect you'd like to come in for a chat?'

Sammi's mum was looking at Kerry earnestly, but he knew she hadn't understood a word she'd said. He felt a bit embarrassed for her. 'She's inviting you inside,' he muttered to her in Pashtun.

They walked up to the big old building. It was *really* old. Sammi stared up at it, wondering if it was something the Victorians had built. Then he pushed the thought away – he wasn't in any hurry to start thinking about the Victorians again. He'd had enough of British history! Inside, he was surprised at how scruffy everything seemed to be. When he'd first arrived in England, he'd expected things to be shiny and new – after all, it was a rich country, wasn't it? But here in the barn there was an old wooden bookshelf, a faded sofa and chairs, and wooden beams showing through the brickwork. He frowned. He wasn't sure he liked it at all.

'Come and meet the team,' said Kerry, leading

them over to an older man who was cradling a mug in his hands. 'This is Rory, the farm manager.'

Rory had a mop of white hair and twinkly blue eyes. He stepped forward to shake his mum's hand, then he bent down and shook Giti's hand too, and finally turned to Sammi.

'Welcome, young Sammi,' he said. 'I know you're a long way from the things you're used to, but you'll do all right here, lad. You'll feel more at home, by and by.'

Sammi liked Rory at once, but he could barely understand a word he said. His English sounded different to anything he'd ever heard before! His mouth opened and closed like a fish as he tried to think of what to say.

Kerry must have understood, because she smiled. 'Rory's from the north of England,' she told Sammi. 'He speaks with a bit of an accent. You'll soon get the hang of it.'

She beckoned a slight girl over from the far end of the barn, where she was arranging a bunch of fresh flowers. The girl stepped back from the vase with her head on one side, checking it over, then skipped across to say hello.

'This is Asha,' Kerry told them. 'She's one of our

volunteers. She comes whenever she's got a spare moment, don't you, Asha?'

'You bet I do,' said Asha, grinning enthusiastically.

Sammi stared at Asha curiously. She was really tiny, and she had really short black hair. She almost looked as though she could be from Afghanistan, but he knew from her voice that she'd grown up here in the UK. And maybe her family had come from somewhere else, anyway, like India or Pakistan.

'Who is this girl?' asked his mum, in Pashtun. She was staring at Asha in curiosity too, and Asha began to look self-conscious.

'She's on the project, like me,' Sammi told her in a low voice. 'Mum, please stop talking in Pashtun.' Sammi was getting mad at her. There was an awkward silence for a second, and Sammi realized that everyone else was waiting for him and his mum to finish their conversation.

'Is Jack around?' Kerry asked Rory.

'He is, but he's still with the goats,' Rory told her.

'Ah well. You'll meet Jack soon enough,' said Kerry, smiling at Sammi. She turned to Asha and Rory. 'We need to have a chat, so why don't you two go and see how many eggs we've got this morning?'

'Sure.' Asha skipped over to the doorway happily.

 24

'See you later, Sammi.' Rory waved and followed her out.

'Right!' Kerry turned to them with a big smile. 'Come and sit down.' She led them over to a desk that was overflowing with papers. Like all the other furniture, it was old and scuffed, and covered with pictures of animals.

'Take a seat,' she said, clearing some papers up from one of the chairs.

Sammi's mum hesitated, looking at Sammi for guidance.

'Sit down, Mum,' Sammi muttered at her. 'It's all right. She told us to.' Mum sank into the chair and pulled Giti onto her lap.

Kerry looked from Sammi to his mum and back again. 'Now, Sammi, I need to talk to your mum, but am I right in thinking she'll need some help?'

Sammi nodded, then shook his head, not sure which was right. 'Her English is not good,' he told her.

'So do you think you can translate for me?'

Sammi nodded.

Kerry looked half at him and half at his mum as she began to speak. 'City Farm is all about helping people,' she said. 'Children are invited to join the Harvest Hope project when they have a problem that's making it hard for them to cope.'

She stopped, and looked at Sammi expectantly. He wasn't sure exactly what she'd said, but he could guess, more or less.

'She's talking about City Farm,' he told his mum. 'She says they try to help people.'

Sammi's mum gave a nervous smile.

'You've been having trouble fitting in at school, haven't you, Sammi?' Kerry carried on. 'We know it's not easy, learning a new language and adjusting to a whole new culture. We hope that spending some time on the farm will help you.'

Sammi shifted from one foot to another, and looked at the ground. 'She says she hopes I'll like it here,' he translated, then decided to change Kerry's words a bit. 'It's a farm with different animals and things to do.'

Now his mum nodded enthusiastically. 'Tell her I'm very happy they sent you here,' she instructed Sammi. 'And you tell her that you're from a good family. You were never in trouble before so there's no reason why you'll cause problems here.' She paused, and gave Sammi a steely look. 'Go on, talk to her nicely. I want you to make a good impression.'

Sammi turned back to Kerry. 'My mum says she

very happy I come here.' Then he stopped. There was no way he'd translate the rest.

Kerry waited, as though she sensed that his mum had said a lot more than that. But Sammi kept his lips shut tight. Kerry hesitated, then reached for a form that she'd filled out. She pointed to a space at the bottom. 'Your mum needs to sign here to show that she's agreed you can be here. Then perhaps she'd like to look around the farm with your little sister before leaving?'

Sammi explained to his mum what to do. 'She says you and Giti can go and look around if you want,' he said.

'Oh, good,' said his mum. 'Giti will love seeing all the animals.' She stood up and reached forward to grasp Kerry by both hands, shaking them warmly. Kerry grinned in return. 'I like this woman,' Sammi's mum told him. 'I can see in her eyes that she's a good person. Tell her thank you a million times for agreeing to look after you.'

'Let go of her hands, Mum,' said Sammi.

'Don't be silly,' said Mum. 'Tell her what I said.'

Sammi turned to Kerry. 'She says thank you,' he said. Then he looked at his mum, and spoke in Pashtun. 'I don't know why you're making such a fuss,' he said. 'I've no idea how this place is going to help me.'

His mum released Kerry's hands and sat down again. 'I don't like you saying things like that, Sammi,' she rebuked him. 'You should be positive about having a new opportunity.'

Sammi pursed his lips. 'That's what you said about school,' he said.

Chapter Three

Sammi's mum took Giti by the hand and led her out of Kerry's office. 'Come on, Giti. We have to leave Sammi now. He's going to be very busy here.'

Giti broke away from her and ran to give Sammi a big hug. 'Bye, Sammi,' she said. 'I want you to teach me everything you learn when you come home.'

'I will,' he promised her, though he knew that Giti wouldn't need teaching. She'd probably learn more from looking around for ten minutes than he'd be able to learn all day.

Giti skipped off with his mum, and he turned back to Kerry. Now that he was on his own, he felt more tongue-tied than ever.

'I won't keep you here long,' said Kerry. 'Just a quick chat before we get you started on the farm.'

 29

Sammi waited.

'Can you explain to me what's been going wrong?' Kerry asked him gently. 'I know you've been finding it hard at school, but your English seems really quite good to me.'

He shook his head. 'It's not,' he said, and lapsed into silence again. He knew that Kerry was hoping he'd say more, but he didn't know what to say. Suddenly, all his English words seemed to have flown out of the window.

'Well, it's a big challenge, learning in another language,' said Kerry eventually. 'Can you understand everything I'm saying to you?'

Sammi shrugged. 'Most,' he said.

'Well, that's something. And you'll soon pick up more, once you're busy working. Practice makes perfect, that's what we say.' Kerry stood up and came around her desk. She placed a hand on Sammi's shoulder and led him out of the barn. 'Most people who come here usually find one special animal to care for,' she told him, as they went outside. 'Which animals do you like best?'

Sammi shrugged again. Even if he could have thought of an animal, he wouldn't know how to describe it in English. He'd seen chickens, but they

 30

didn't need much looking after. He'd heard a sheep somewhere, but he only knew the word in Pashtun.

'Well, perhaps you can start by looking at the rabbits and guinea pigs,' said Kerry. 'I'll find Jack to show you where they are, and what we do for them each day.'

They started off down a garden path. Sammi wondered what sort of animals they were going to see. He hadn't understood either of the words that Kerry had said. *Rab-bit, gwidypig.* He rolled the words round in his head, trying to remember them.

The garden was really pretty, with lots of lush vegetables growing. It reminded Sammi of his grandmother's garden in Afghanistan, where she'd grown lots of onions and spinach and herbs. There had been lots of grape vines growing at the bottom half of it, but he couldn't see anything like that here. He felt a pang of sadness. She had died not long before they were forced to leave their village – not long after his dad had disappeared. They'd had to leave her house behind, so there was no saying what had happened to it.

'Sammi?' said Kerry. 'We're going this way.'

Sammi realized he'd stopped walking, and was lost in his own thoughts, back in the village with his family. He tried to concentrate again as Kerry pointed out an old apple tree at the bottom of the garden, and a pond with ducks quacking around it. Then she spotted a boy of about Sammi's age, busy digging something in one of the vegetable patches.

'Jack!' she called. 'Can you come over, please?'

The boy had his back to them, but he stuck his spade in the ground right away and brushed some mud off his shirt. Sammi frowned. There was something strangely familiar about him.

'Jack, this is Sammi,' Kerry was saying. 'He's the new member of the Harvest Hope project. Would you mind helping him to settle in? I thought you could take him to see the rabbits and guinea pigs – could you show him how to feed them and clean them out?'

The boy was closer now, and Sammi could see his face, his sandy hair and his freckles. His heart sank. He didn't need an introduction because he knew exactly who he was. He was the boy from his class, the one whose books he'd knocked to the floor. The boy who'd looked really cross about it. The one he'd gone and called 'Stupid'…

Jack got a bit of a shock when he saw Sammi. Kerry had told him about an Afghan boy arriving on the Harvest Hope project, but he'd never imagined it'd be the boy in his class! Sammi had gone bright red. Jack stared at him, thinking about what had happened in class. He hadn't liked him much, right from the start – he'd always been rude and moody, never bothering to answer Miss Crawley properly. Then he'd caused a right scene, storming out and knocking all Jack's books down ... And he couldn't believe what he'd actually *said*!

The thing that Jack hated more than anything else was people thinking he was stupid. It got him really mad. Yes, he was in the bottom class – because he had dyslexia, so he had problems with reading and writing. But that didn't make him stupid, did it? It was just really frustrating. Not long after starting at this school, a bunch of boys had started teasing him about it, calling him stupid, a dimwit, the village idiot, and all kinds of things. He'd got into big trouble by shouting back at them.

He could see that Kerry was expecting him to be welcoming, so he tried to smile.

'Hi, Sammi,' he said, but he knew it had come out funny.

Sammi looked at the ground, then looked away. 'Hi,' he muttered.

There was an awkward silence.

 33

Kerry looked at them curiously. 'Have you two met each other before?' she asked.

'Er … yeah,' said Jack. 'We're in the same English class at school. It's the bottom one because … well, you know.'

'Ah. Yes, I understand.'

Jack sensed that Kerry was studying his face. He looked up and met her gaze, and saw at once that she'd spotted the awkwardness between himself and Sammi.

'Well, Jack, this is a chance to make a fresh start,' she said, looking at him very directly. 'Everyone gets a second chance on the Harvest Hope project, don't they?'

He nodded reluctantly. 'I guess.'

She was telling him to make an effort, he knew that. After all, he'd been difficult himself when he first arrived at City Farm, angry with everyone and everything. But underneath, he'd been really missing his grandad and the farm he'd grown up on. He'd hated everything about the city, especially the bullies at school, and it was only Harvest Hope that had helped him start enjoying himself again.

'I'll leave you to it, then,' said Kerry.

'OK,' agreed Jack.

 34

Kerry headed back towards the barn, leaving Sammi at Jack's side. Sammi looked just the way he did in class – angry and silent. Jack tried not to let it bother him, and pointed along one of the paths.

'The rabbits are this way,' he said, and set off, leading the way past Rory the Second, the garden scarecrow. He was about to explain to Sammi, but then decided against it. There wasn't much point – Sammi wouldn't understand, anyway.

They reached the rabbit and guinea pig hutches, sitting side by side.

'Which d'you want to do first?' asked Jack. 'There's four rabbits – Peaches and Cream, and Crumble and Custard. There's two guinea pigs, Bubble and Squeak.'

Sammi shrugged. He didn't look very interested in either of them.

Bubble and Squeak, the two guinea pigs, had already started squealing, which they always did if they thought there was any chance of food.

'Weeee! Weeee-ee!' peeped Squeak, with her little nose up in the air.

'OK. Well, I prefer the guinea pigs. I love the noises they make,' said Jack. 'D'you want to hold one first?'

'*Hold* one?' Sammi looked startled.

 35

'Yeah, you can, if you want.' Jack went through the little gate. Squeak poked her nose out of the guinea pig run, her squealing sound louder than ever. 'They know it's feeding time. Listen to them!'

He picked Squeak up and stroked her for a moment, ruffling up her soft fur. Then he handed her to Sammi.

Sammi looked confused, and held Squeak awkwardly. 'What I do with him?'

'It's not a him. It's a her,' said Jack. 'You don't have to do anything with her. Most people like picking them up, that's all. You can stroke her – she enjoys that.'

Sammi frowned. He carried on holding Squeak far out in front of him like she smelled bad. He obviously wasn't interested in stroking her. Jack sighed. 'Give her back here, then,' he said. 'We'll go and get them some feed.'

With Squeak safely back in her run, Sammi trailed after Jack to the feed room.

'We can feed the rabbits at the same time,' said Jack. 'But you have to be careful. Their food looks similar, but it's a bit different. The guinea pig food has vitamin C in it, 'cause they can't store it in their bodies the way rabbits do.'

He was quite proud of his knowledge, and he looked at Sammi's face, trying to work out whether he'd followed what he was saying. It was hard to tell. Jack handed over the rabbit feed and carried the guinea pig feed himself, then led the way back out into the garden.

'We give a handful of carrots and lettuces to the rabbits,' said Jack. 'The guinea pigs will eat carrots, but they like plenty of normal grass too. And dandelion leaves, they go nuts for them!'

They made their way back to the hutches and put all the food in the right bowls, then went and collected some vegetables, grass and dandelion leaves from the garden. Jack showed Sammi how to check the water supply, and how to clean the droppings out of the cages. Sammi watched him, but he didn't try to join in.

What's wrong with him? Jack wondered. Most people thought the rabbits and guinea pigs were gorgeous, even boys! But Sammi didn't seem the least bit interested in them. He just kept scuffing his shoe against the hutch, looking bored. *Maybe he thinks he's too cool to work with animals*, thought Jack. He was running out of things to say. He was fed up. He'd done his best with Sammi, hadn't he? He'd really tried to help, even though Sammi had been so mean to him. He'd pretty much had enough.

'That's it,' he said, once he'd finished the cleaning.

 37

'It's simple, really. There's nothing else to do.'

Sammi nodded. 'OK.'

'So … I have to go and finish my other jobs. You can just look around, if you want.'

'OK.'

Jack stared at him. Was that all he could say? '*OK*'?

'Right. Well, see you later then.' He raised a hand. 'Don't tell me − *OK*.'

Sammi looked at him blankly, then shrugged. Jack turned away. It was too bad. Sammi hadn't made any kind of effort with the animals, or tried to make up for what had happened in class. Jack had done his best. It wasn't his fault if Sammi wasn't interested. He walked off, shaking his head. There was just no helping some people.

Jack went back to the vegetable patch in the garden and started digging up some potatoes so that Bea, the lady who worked in the farm café, could make some potato salad. It was hard work, plunging the big fork into the soil then lifting it out − a great job to do when you were feeling cross! He shook the dirt off the neat round potatoes, and didn't stop until he'd filled up a basket. Then he headed up to the barn.

Inside, Asha was on the sofa, sitting very still. Jack stared at her. Asha *never* sat still. She was a ball of energy, always charging around, full of enthusiasm. She was on the Harvest Hope project to help her recover from leukaemia, but Jack sometimes thought she was more likely to wear herself out!

'What's wrong?' he demanded.

Asha nodded towards Kerry's desk. Jack put his basket down, and listened. He could hear that Kerry was on the phone, trying to get a word in with someone. And she was finding it very difficult.

'I do appreciate that, but … Yes, but the point is … No, no. I don't think—'

Kerry's voice rose higher each time she tried to speak, as she grew more frustrated.

Jack frowned at Asha. 'Who is it?' he asked.

Asha looked close to despair. 'Derrick Jarvis. From the council.'

Jack rolled his eyes. Derrick Jarvis was always causing trouble. 'Not him again,' he said.

'Jack, I'm worried,' said Asha. 'It's serious this time. Really serious. He was here when I arrived yesterday, and he had all these men with him, and they were talking about building houses on City Farm. He said they're cutting the funding. Kerry says we might have to close.'

'They can't do that!' exclaimed Jack.

 39

'Well, that's the trouble. I'm really scared. Kerry says they can.'

Jack suddenly felt very funny, as though his whole world was spinning around him. Memories rushed through his head. He remembered the day they'd told him that his grandad couldn't manage the farm any more, and that they'd have to move to the city. It had been the saddest day of his life. Well, almost – the day they'd actually left had been even sadder.

He sat down on an armchair with a bump. He'd lost one life he loved – he couldn't bear it if he lost his life at City Farm too.

Kerry finally banged the phone down and came through into the main room.

'That man is *so* unreasonable!' she exclaimed.

'What's happening?' demanded Jack. 'Asha says they're going to shut us down!'

'Not if I can help it,' said Kerry grimly. 'We'll fight it with everything we have. Don't worry, Jack – it hasn't happened yet.'

Jack felt a rush of relief. Of course, Kerry and Rory wouldn't let it happen. They always made everything work out all right.

Then Kerry looked at him. 'Jack, where's Sammi?'

'Sammi?' Jack shrugged. 'He's out on the farm

somewhere.'

'What do you mean, somewhere? I thought you were helping him with the rabbits?'

Jack felt defensive. 'He wasn't interested in them. We fed them and cleaned them out and stuff, but … he just didn't seem bothered.'

'So you've left him on his own? What's he doing now?'

Jack suddenly realized what he'd done. He'd abandoned Sammi to look after himself – and Kerry had asked him specially to help him settle in. 'I don't know.' He hardly dared looked at Asha and Kerry's faces.

'Jack, it's his first day.' Kerry's voice was gentle, but disappointed too.

'I know.' Jack jumped to his feet. 'I'll go right back – I'll just take these potatoes to the kitchen—'

Kerry looked at him kindly. 'I could see that you two have a problem. I suppose it's something that happened at school, and you haven't managed to sort it out. That's all right, Jack. You can't be friends with everybody. But you should have come to talk to me if you weren't getting along. It's very hard for Sammi – he's lost everything he's ever known. His whole life. We have to be patient with him, don't you think?'

 41

Jack felt wretched. He of all people knew all about losing the life he loved. He hung his head. 'I'm really sorry, Kerry.'

'OK. We all make mistakes.' Kerry smiled her lovely warm smile. 'I know what – we'll all go together to find him. City Farm is all about finding solutions together, isn't it?'

Asha was still looking glum. 'Derrick Jarvis doesn't seem to think so,' she said.

'We'll show Derrick Jarvis what we're made of,' said Kerry. 'You wait and see.'

Chapter Four

When Jack left him standing by the rabbit hutches, Sammi felt quite relieved. It had all been very awkward. He didn't like the idea of touching little furry animals – they never did it back home. The guinea pigs reminded him of rats, more than anything, and rats were nothing but pests! Jack clearly thought he was rude, boring and a pain, but that was nothing new. Everyone at that stupid school seemed to see him that way.

Thinking about school made him feel miserable. He wandered off down the path that led back towards the pond, kicking stones as he went. It was quiet there, apart from the ducks quacking and swimming around, and a couple of geese preening their feathers. He squatted down and watched as a dragonfly hovered over one of the big round waterlily leaves that rested on the surface of the water. He sighed. This place was nice, but it was so, so different from Afghanistan. He couldn't imagine ever feeling at home here.

Suddenly, he heard a sound. A kind of strange hissing noise. He looked around and saw a massive white bird coming towards him across the surface of the water. It was enormous! It had a long, snaky neck and a big black bill, and it definitely meant business. Sammi had never seen anything like it before!

He got to his feet like a shot. The bird had its huge white wings spread wide. It ran over the water at him, and Sammi panicked. He turned around and ran away as fast as he could. He had no idea where he was going, but he had to get out of there!

He bolted around the garden and up through all the flower beds. There was a woman on one of the pathways with a basket of flowers on her arm, and he accidentally knocked it as he rushed past.

'Hey! Careful! Slow down!' yelled the woman. 'No running on the pathways!'

Sammi glanced back, and saw that he'd spilled half the flowers. The woman was bending over picking them up. *Not again*, he thought to himself. All he seemed to do was cause trouble! He couldn't bear it.

He raced on until he was out of sight, then dived into one of the sheds. To his relief, there was no one in there. He didn't want to have to deal with anyone else being cross with him.

He leaned against some of the sacks, trying to get his breath back. He felt awful. He thought of what his mum had said, just before leaving: *I want you to make a good impression.* His heart was beating painfully in his chest. He'd let her down. He'd made a terrible impression at school, and now he'd made a terrible impression at City Farm as well. He thought of how he'd been in Afghanistan: all his friends had loved him for being good fun, and the adults loved him because he was happy and helpful, and just a little bit cheeky, but not too much.

That Sammi had disappeared now. Everything had changed. Life in the UK was a disaster.

He heard footsteps outside the feed room, and held his breath. He didn't want anyone to find him in here. The person passed by, and Sammi peered outside. There was no one in sight, so he tiptoed out and looked around. Just beyond the sheds, he spotted a couple of small fields. Maybe there'd be something more interesting there? He thought about the sheep he'd heard when he arrived – maybe he could go and look for that. Much better to see some real farm animals, instead of silly pet fluffy things, and hopefully there wouldn't be any more big white birds to scare the pants off him!

He walked over to the fields, looking over his shoulder every now and again to check he wasn't being watched. There were some sheep in the first field – but they were nothing like sheep he'd seen before. They were kind of rounder and shorter, and they had floppy fringes over their eyes.

'Weird,' he said to himself.

He moved on to the next field, and saw a black and white pony grazing alongside a big gingery-coloured horse. Sammi watched them for a moment. The pony raised his head and looked at him, then carried on munching grass. Sammi was soon bored, and was about to turn away when he noticed something else, standing in the shade of a big leafy tree. This time it was something very familiar. It was a donkey.

He hadn't even thought about it before, but this was the first donkey he'd seen since leaving Afghanistan. Now he realized he'd missed all the donkey carts and donkey noises that had been part of life back home. He remembered the sun slanting through the dust, the rattle of wooden carts, and the clip-clop of hooves on the dry, narrow streets … all so different to this little green field. But the donkey was just like donkeys everywhere, with his big face and grey coat with the stripe running down the middle of his back, and another stripe running down his shoulder.

He vaulted over the fence and made his way over.

'Hello,' he greeted him, in Pashtun.

The donkey was watching him approach. As he got closer, he raised his head and began to bray noisily, showing all his big yellow teeth. Sammi paused for a moment. He didn't feel at all afraid, but he wanted the donkey to get a good look at him before he went any closer.

'Ee-yore, eeee-yore!' bellowed the donkey. He was really loud!

Sammi grinned, then stepped closer and held out his hand. The donkey stopped braying. His ears pricked forward, and he stretched out his neck. He flared his nostrils and sniffed Sammi's hand.

'Good boy,' murmured Sammi. 'You're the first donkey I've met here, did you know that?'

He took another step forward so that he could stroke the donkey's soft muzzle, then his big, fluffy ears. He ran a hand down his neck and felt surprised at how velvety his coat was. Back home, donkeys had to work hard, and they didn't have much lush grass to eat. He thought of how the donkey boys beat them to make them go faster. This one had a very nice life compared to them.

'You're a lucky donkey, did you know that?' he whispered. 'I'm supposed to feel lucky too, living here in the UK. But I don't. It's awful. I just wish I could go home.'

The donkey stood quietly, then nudged at Sammi's pockets, looking for treats.

Sammi laughed. 'There's nothing there, silly,' he said. 'But never mind. You're much better than the rabbits. Maybe I'll bring you a treat next time – if I ever come back.'

He thought of the woman's flowers and the way she'd yelled about not running. Then he thought about Jack, and how he'd given up on him so easily. He began to feel very gloomy, and leaned his head against the donkey's neck.

The donkey twitched his ears and nudged him again. Sammi straightened up and scratched his neck, just below his mane, working his way right up to his ears. The donkey snorted, clearly enjoying the attention.

'I suppose it wouldn't be too bad here, if I could spend my time with you,' Sammi told him.

But that was the trouble. Kerry had said he should look after the stupid rabbits and guinea pigs. If he came back, he bet she'd make him do that every single weekend, wouldn't she? And he'd probably be made to apologize to Jack, then that woman with the flowers, and it would all be ten times worse than being at school.

He'd have to talk to his mum. He wasn't coming back.

Suddenly the donkey shifted and pricked his ears, looking at something. Then, just as he'd done when Sammi came into the field, he started to bray.

'Ee-yore! Eeee-yore!' he screeched.

Sammi followed the donkey's gaze. To his dismay, he wasn't alone any more. There were three people watching him. Kerry, Jack and Asha were all there, leaning over the gate. He felt his heart begin to race. Now he'd be in huge trouble for everything he'd done! He wished there was somewhere to run, but there was nowhere to go.

For one instant, his dad's face popped into his mind. He tried to imagine what he'd say: '*Be brave, son, and face up to them.*'

Then he felt the donkey butting his arm again, and snorted. Sammi looked into his soft brown eyes. It was almost as though he was trying to say, 'Go on. You can do it!'

'All right, donkey,' he muttered. 'I'm going.'

He gave the soft grey neck one last pat, then slowly turned away and walked towards the gate.

Chapter Five

Asha watched as Sammi sauntered towards them. His hands were in his pockets and he looked more grumpy than ever. She felt a little bit sorry for Jack, because she could see exactly how difficult it would be to keep trying to be friendly with someone who looked so cross. No wonder he'd come and found Dusty the donkey – they were as grumpy as each other!

But then she noticed something else. Dusty had left the shade of the tree. He was following Sammi – and he wasn't braying! In fact, he looked quite eager, with his ears pricked forward and a little spring in his stride.

'Sammi!' she called. 'Look behind you! Dusty's following you!'

The boy looked back at the donkey plodding behind him. And now Dusty raised his head and started braying again at the top of his voice.

'EE-yore! EEEE-yore!'

Asha put her hands over her ears. Dusty was so loud, and when he brayed it was as though he was warning everyone to stay well away from him. But Sammi didn't seem to mind at all. He turned around and placed his hand on Dusty's neck. Dusty stopped braying at once, and stood patiently as Sammi patted and stroked him.

Asha was amazed. 'How did you do that?' she asked excitedly.

She let herself into the field, with Jack and Kerry behind her. Sammi looked wary, and a little hunched, almost as though he was expecting them all to tell him off.

'I not hurt him,' he said in a defensive voice.

'Of course you're not hurting him! He likes you!' laughed Asha.

Sammi was studying everyone's faces. He looked puzzled. 'You are not angry?' he asked, glancing up at Kerry.

'Angry? No, of course not! It looks like you've just made a friend!' smiled Kerry.

Asha saw relief spread over Sammi's face. So he *had* thought they were annoyed with him! But why?

He hadn't done anything wrong. She suddenly felt sorry for him, and realized how hard it must be when there was so much that you didn't understand.

She still wasn't quite sure that she wanted to get close to Dusty though. She stood a couple of paces away while Sammi continued to stroke him. 'Dusty never stands quietly for me. He just scares me with his big yellow teeth and all the noise he makes! He's so grumpy.'

Sammi frowned. 'He is what?' he asked quietly. 'What this word?'

'Grumpy! Um, it means…' Asha looked round to Kerry for help.

Kerry pulled a long, cross face, and made a growly, bad-tempered sound. 'This is grumpy,' she explained.

Asha copied her, and tried to make a grumpy donkey sound too. 'Grumpy means … not happy,' she explained. 'He doesn't like other people. He's always in a bad mood!'

Understanding slowly spread across Sammi's face. He looked from Asha to Kerry, and repeated the word slowly, trying to get the sound right. 'Groompy. Graampy. No. Grumpy. Gru*m*py. Is a good word.' He smiled slightly. 'But this donkey is not grumpy. He is trying to say hello.'

He placed his head close to Dusty's, then imitated his braying sound. 'Hel-lo … Hel-lo…!'

Asha giggled. Sammi could really be quite funny, when he started to relax.

'Donkeys not speak English either,' Sammi said. 'I think this donkey like to have friends.'

'Oh! I wish you'd arrived here sooner,' said Asha, laughing. 'Just think – all this time, Dusty was just trying to be friendly, and we didn't know what he was saying!'

Sammi met her gaze. He looked sad, and she realized that maybe the same thing was true for him too. She smiled at him warmly. 'Let's take him into the yard,' she said. 'I'll show you where we keep all the grooming things. You can brush him down – he'll love that.'

But now the bad-tempered look was back on Sammi's face. He glanced at Kerry. 'My job is not donkey,' he said. 'I think rabbits.'

'No, no, that's all right, Sammi,' said Kerry. 'Don't worry about the rabbits. It's more important for you to work with an animal that really interests you.'

Sammi looked shocked, as though he hadn't quite got what she said. But then he worked it out, and his face split into a real smile for the first time. He stared at Dusty in disbelief. 'I can … um … look after the donkey?' he asked.

'Yes, you look after Dusty,' said Kerry. 'Dusty's just as happy as you are! Aren't you, Dusty?'

Dusty raised his head and brayed again.

'I think he say yes,' smiled Sammi.

Asha fetched a head collar from the storerooms, and, feeling a little bit nervous, she helped Sammi put it over Dusty's big ears. She half expected Dusty to snap at her with his big teeth, but with Sammi soothing him, he stayed calm and gentle. As they led him through to the yard, Dusty 'eeee-yored' once, but he soon stopped when Sammi made a fuss of him. Asha grinned as she realized that the donkey just wanted people to notice him a bit more!

It had been so nice to see Sammi and Dusty getting along so well that she'd almost forgotten about Derrick Jarvis. Now she decided not to think about his horrible threats, and focus on helping Sammi instead. She fetched the box with all the grooming kit in it.

'This is a body brush,' she explained, fishing one out. 'We use this to brush the horses all over. They really like it. You can use it on Dusty too.'

Sammy frowned, and took the brush without a

word. For a moment, Asha thought he'd gone back to being silent again. But then she realized that he'd just been trying to follow what she said, and he was frowning because he was concentrating.

She took another body brush from the box and showed him what to do. 'We use big, strong strokes – like this,' she told him, brushing Dusty's neck.

Sammi nodded, and copied her actions. Soon he was hard at work, brushing Dusty from top to toe.

'He's not noisy now,' he said, after a while. 'He much happy, I think!'

Asha laughed. 'You're right,' she said. 'And I think maybe you're happier too, Sammi?'

Sammi smiled at her. 'Yes, it true,' he agreed. 'Dusty make me feel like home.'

'Home? You mean Afghanistan?' Asha hesitated. 'Do you miss it very much?'

Sammi nodded. 'It's very different there.' He grinned. 'Many donkeys.'

'Did you have a donkey of your own there?' asked Asha.

'No. My cousin have one.' Sammi stopped stroking Dusty for a moment. 'My cousin die in the war. I not know what happen to the donkey.'

'Oh! I'm so sorry.' Asha remembered what Kerry

had said about his dad. It was hard to imagine the terrible things that Sammi and his family had left behind.

She hesitated. 'Is some of your family still there?' she asked, a bit awkwardly.

'My father.' Sammi didn't look at Asha as he spoke. He had bent down to brush some mud from Dusty's back legs, but she could still hear the sadness in his voice. 'Also my big sister, and her baby. But I will work to make money, and one day they come here,' he finished determinedly.

'Oh, I hope so!' said Asha. 'It must have been really hard, leaving them out there.'

'Yes. But my sister is strong. Very stubborn.' Sammi peeped over Dusty's back, and now there was a twinkle in his eye. 'She always tell me off before. Now she can't. She too far away!'

Asha grinned back. She knew it wasn't easy, keeping cheerful about things that were painful.

They carried on working for a while, until their arms ached. Sammi stopped for a minute and leaned against Dusty's sturdy shoulder.

'Asha,' he said. 'I have question.'

'Go on,' said Asha.

'There is big bird here,' said Sammi. 'Very big bird.

White. I think very dangerous. It come after me saying "sssss, sssss".' He wiggled his neck, imitating it.

Asha giggled. 'Oh, that's just one of the swans!' she said. 'Don't you have them in Afghanistan?'

Sammi shook his head. 'I not know. I never see one.'

'I expect it was trying to fly – they look really silly as they run across the water.' Asha explained. 'They're not dangerous though, although they get a bit protective when they've got eggs or cygnets.'

'They what?'

'Cyg-nets.' Asha said it slowly. 'Their babies.'

'I no see babies. But maybe it try fly? I run. I run very fast. I make accident with lady in garden. I think she very angry with me now, I make her fall flowers on the ground, but I sorry, I afraid this big bird, I think it try kill me...' Sammi's words were suddenly tumbling out all in a rush, as though he was making a big confession.

'You say a lady was picking flowers in the garden?' asked Asha.

'Yes. But they all go...' Sammi flopped his hands over, showing how they'd fallen.

'Oh, that's just Bea. She works in the cafe, and picks flowers for the tables every morning,' said Asha. She smiled brightly. 'You needn't worry about her, Sammi. She's really lovely and friendly. She won't be angry with you at all – especially when she hears about your adventure with the swan!'

'Oh.' Sammi calmed down. 'Is OK then?'

Poor Sammi, thought Asha. His first day hadn't gone very well at all. First he and Jack hadn't got on, and then he'd been frightened by the swan, and then he'd bumped into Bea … no wonder he'd been looking so gloomy.

'Everything's all right,' she said. 'It's absolutely fine.'

And she was determined that everything would be, from now on!

Chapter Six

When Sammi woke up the next Saturday, he felt different. Usually, and always on school days, he wanted to hide his head under the duvet and go back to sleep. But today he knew there was something to look forward to. What was it? He sat upright in bed. That was it – City Farm, and Dusty the donkey! He jumped out of bed and got ready as fast as he could. It was a beautiful sunny day, and he didn't want to waste any of it!

There was just one thing he didn't want to forget. Before leaving the house, he checked in the fridge for vegetables.

'What are you looking for?' demanded his mum.

'Carrots,' said Sammi. 'I promised the donkey I'd take him a treat.'

 60

His mum looked as though he'd gone mad. 'The *donkey*!' she exclaimed.

'All the animals at City Farm get treats,' said Sammi. 'Please, Mum!'

His mum rolled her eyes, then smiled. 'It's good to see you looking happier, Sammi,' she said. 'There's a bag of carrots right in the bottom drawer. Don't take all of them though, we need some for *our* dinner!'

Sammi grinned. He grabbed a couple and stuffed them into his pocket, then headed for the door. 'See you later!' he called, and ran out to catch the bus.

Once he'd arrived at City Farm, he let himself in through the big iron gates and went straight round to Dusty's field. Dusty was grazing, but he heard Sammi coming and immediately gave an enormous 'Ee-yore!'

'All right, all right, Dusty,' said Sammi, in Pashtun. 'You can stop making such a noise now.'

The donkey came over to the fence, still braying. Sammi let himself into the field and went to meet him, patting him on the neck and stroking his soft grey nose. Dusty's ears were pricked.

'I know what you can smell!' laughed Sammi. He reached into his pocket and fetched out one of the carrots. 'Here you are.'

Dusty gobbled the carrot greedily. Then he started

nosing Sammi's pockets for more.

'No more just yet,' Sammi told him. 'I'm saving that for later!' He left Dusty in the field, and went to fetch the long rope so that he could bring him in to the yard. To his surprise, there were three men standing by the storeroom. They didn't look like they belonged on the farm, because they wore yellow hard hats and bright yellow fluorescent jackets.

One of them had a big tape measure in one hand, and a clipboard in the other. 'I reckon we start at the far end,' he was saying. 'Over by the field there.'

'Good idea,' said another. 'I'll take one end of the tape—'

'Oh no, you don't!' bellowed a voice. 'You're not starting anywhere!'

Sammi spun round. Rory the farm manager was marching towards the men, his white hair standing up wildly and his wrinkled face bright red.

'You have no right to be here!' Rory shouted. 'No one's signed any papers yet! You get out of our farm!'

The men looked startled, and backed off a little bit. 'But we're from the council…' one of them began.

'Well, you go right back to the council!' roared Rory. 'And don't you dare set foot here again without the correct papers!'

 62

'We're just trying to save everyone time,' said another of the men. 'If we can just get the site measured up...'

'*Waste* everyone's time, more like!' Rory was really angry. 'We haven't given our consent for any of this. You'll see – City Farm will stay just the way it is!'

The men were looking uneasy. They began to make their way to the car park in the front yard, with Rory ushering them forwards. Sammi followed them, feeling curious. He couldn't work out what was happening – why was Rory so angry?

'We're going for now,' said one of the men, as he got into his car. 'But you should know the council's position. As far as we're concerned, City Farm will close on Sunday October the twelfth. And that's final, I'm afraid.'

'It will do nothing of the sort!' said Rory. 'And now, please leave!'

Sammi's mouth dropped open. City Farm – close? But why? He watched as the men started the engine, and screeched out of the gates.

When they had gone, Rory's anger disappeared. His shoulders sagged, and he looked terribly sad. Sammi thought he seemed ten years older.

'Is this true?' asked Sammi. 'They close City Farm?'

 63

'I'm afraid so, lad,' said Rory, his voice quiet now. 'We'll do our best to save it, but you heard what they said. Time's running out. October the twelfth…' His voice drifted, and he looked into the distance, as though his whole life was falling away.

A thought occurred to Sammi. 'Where animals go, if it close?' he asked.

Rory looked sadder than ever. 'That's a very good question,' he replied. 'We don't know. We'll have to find new homes for all of them, or they'll be homeless.' He gave a big, heavy sigh. 'And, for that matter, so will I.'

'You?' Sammi wondered if he'd understood properly.

'I live here, lad,' said Rory. He waved towards an old farmhouse, tucked behind the barn. 'This is my home. Has been for years. If the animals go, I go too. It's the end of City Farm.'

'But this very bad.' Sammi shook his head.

'It's bad, all right,' nodded Rory. 'But the way things are going, there may not be much we can do about it.'

Sammi went back to Dusty's field feeling shocked. He had imagined that England was a very safe place, where no one ever lost their home. Now he realized that things could change here too, and he felt sorry for

Rory and all the animals.

He was just bringing Dusty into the yard when Asha appeared. He could tell from her face that she wasn't feeling happy. Maybe she'd heard the news about the farm too.

'Hi, Sammi,' she said. 'How are you today?'

'Me, I am fine,' said Sammi. 'I think City Farm not fine.'

Asha looked as though she might burst into tears. 'No, it's not,' she agreed. 'We're going to have a meeting to talk about it soon. Would you like to come?'

'Yes, I come!' said Sammi at once. 'I just give Dusty food.'

'Oh, yes,' said Asha. 'There's no hurry, we've all got chores to do first. Come when you've finished with Dusty.'

'I come,' repeated Sammi.

He led Dusty into the stall that Asha had shown him and fetched the donkey some fresh hay from the feed room. Dusty snorted happily, and began pulling at his hay net. Sammi brought him a bucket of fresh water, then watched him for a moment. He was thinking. In Afghanistan, he'd ridden his cousin's donkey many, many times.

'How would you feel about having a rider, Dusty?'

he asked the donkey, in Pashtun.

Dusty flicked his ears to and fro lazily. He was completely relaxed. Sammi placed a hand on his neck. Dusty turned from his hay to butt Sammi's arm affectionately. Sammi grinned. He placed one hand on the donkey's mane and jumped lightly onto his back. Dusty stopped eating and took a few steps back in surprise.

'It's OK, it's OK,' Sammi murmured to him. 'It's only me.'

Dusty stood quietly, then snorted again. Sammi reached forward and scratched him, all the way up to the ears. Then he lay down along his neck and hugged him, and Dusty turned his head back, his ears pricked in curiosity.

'Good boy,' said Sammi happily. He slid back down to the ground. 'I'll give you a proper ride next time, out in the field. You'll like that!' he told the donkey.

Dusty was still calm and happy. He hadn't 'ee-yored' noisily at all this morning. He went back to his hay net, and carried on munching. Sammi felt a buzz of excitement. He and Dusty were going to have so much fun! After one last pat, he left his friend reluctantly, and headed up to the barn.

Asha and Jack were already inside, sitting on the

sofa, with Rory in one of the armchairs and other people dotted around. Sammi scanned the room for somewhere to sit, and spotted a familiar face. *Oh, no!* he thought. All at once, his nerves came flooding back. It was Bea, the cafe worker – the one who'd been picking the flowers…

Shame washed over him. He lowered his gaze and began to inch his way across the room.

But to his surprise, Bea called him. 'Come on in, Sammi!' she cried. 'Asha's explained all about that big old swan. She's a tricky one, she is. Enough to frighten the life out of anyone! Come, come.' She patted the seat next to her. 'You'll be just fine here!'

Sammi looked up at her timidly. Bea had warm brown eyes, and round rosy cheeks that looked like little red apples when she smiled. Asha was right. She really did look friendly!

'Yes, yes, make yourself comfortable, Sammi,' said Kerry, appearing from her office. 'You're just in time. We're about to begin.'

Sammi perched on the edge of the chair next to Bea. In spite of everyone's welcome, he felt a little bit self-conscious. He'd only visited City Farm twice – surely he wasn't important enough to take part in the meeting? He wasn't even sure if he'd be able to understand everything.

But once everyone started talking, he understood only too well. There was one big problem. It was as the council men had said: unless they were able to find a solution very fast, City Farm would close on Sunday 12 October – just two weeks from now.

'We must let the whole community know,' said Bea. 'City Farm is really popular. If everyone knew what the council was planning, they'd be really shocked! They'd never let it happen.'

'We should have a demonstration – a protest march!' said Jack.

'Yes! Yes!' Asha leaped at the idea. 'That's a brilliant idea, Jack! I'll chain myself to the City Farm gates! Or ... or ... maybe I'll go on hunger strike! Or why not both? I could chain myself up and be on a hunger strike at the same time!'

'Steady on, lass,' said Rory. 'There's little enough of you as it is.'

'But we have to do something dramatic!' cried Asha. 'I can't *bear* for the farm to close.'

Kerry smiled at Asha's enthusiasm. 'Well, I really appreciate that you want to make an impact, Asha,' she said. 'But I think we can do that without you chaining yourself up. Or starving yourself. We just need to let the council know that City Farm is very important to the community – too important to close.'

'So how do we do that?' asked Jack.

'Well – one way would be a petition,' said Kerry. 'If lots of people sign, saying that they value the farm and want it to stay open, the council will be placed in a difficult position.'

'Aye. But we need people to show their faces too,' said Rory. 'We need open support. I say we get everyone who supports us to come here on October the twelfth. If there's enough of us, they won't dare close us down.'

'Oh! I know hundreds of people who'll come!' exclaimed Asha. 'All the people from my school, and all the people I met in hospital, and everyone from my mum's work, and my dad's work, and we can ask Laura to bring everyone from the Braille school, and then there's my swimming club…'

'Yes, that's exactly the right idea,' said Kerry. 'I'm sure we can all think of groups of people we can ask. But we can ask strangers too – people in the community nearby who know about the farm and have perhaps visited it.'

Sammi sat listening. He understood more or less what was going on. He didn't know what 'petition' was, but he gathered they were discussing all the people who might be able to save the farm. He had known so many people in Afghanistan, but he knew hardly anyone here. Just his uncle, his mum, and his little sister Giti. Who else was there? No one. He began to feel miserable again. His two days at City Farm had been his happiest for a long time, but they were coming to an end almost before they'd started.

Kerry disappeared into her office for a few moments, and came back with some neatly printed sheets.

'Here we are,' she announced. 'I've made some petition sheets. It says at the top, "We wish the council to know that City Farm is a much-loved and valuable part of our community. Its closure is against our wishes and we demand that the council reconsider its decision." Then there are rows for people to write their names and put their signature. Is that OK?'

'Perfect,' said Rory.

'And we can invite everyone who signs the petition to come and join us on the twelfth. Even if we don't succeed, we'll have brought the community together one last time,' said Kerry.

'Oh, but it has to succeed!' cried Asha. 'When the council see how many people love it here, they'll never be able to close us down!'

'You could be right, lass,' said Rory. 'Here, Kerry, let me give those out to everybody.'

Rory stood up and began to hand out the petition sheets. Sammi could feel his heart beating faster as he took one. There was no way he could help. Why did life have to be so difficult? He'd only just started settling into City Farm, and now he'd been given something he couldn't do. He felt almost panicky. He didn't know anyone who would sign. He had to get out of it somehow … Ideas raced through his head. Maybe he could pretend to sign lots of names himself. But he didn't know many English names, and his English letters were still wobbly and babyish. *Think of something. Think of an excuse*, he said to himself. But his mind was completely blank. He was stuck. What on earth was he going to do?

Chapter Seven

As soon as the meeting was over, Sammi stuffed the petition into his bag. He didn't want to think about it. He would go out and spend time with Dusty while he still could – while City Farm was still open.

He was about to sneak out of the barn when Kerry called him.

'Sammi – would you come here for a minute?'

Dragging his feet, Sammi went over to her desk.

Kerry smiled kindly at him. 'Thank you for taking a petition sheet, Sammi,' she said. 'Do you understand what it's for?'

'I understand,' said Sammi. 'City Farm need help. But I don't…' His voice trailed off, and he shrugged. He didn't know how to explain.

'I think I can guess what you're thinking. You feel

that you don't know enough people,' Kerry finished for him.

Sammi stared at her in surprise. She'd guessed exactly right! He nodded.

'That's OK, Sammi,' said Kerry. 'But think about it. You have neighbours, don't you?'

'I not know them.'

'You don't know them *yet*,' said Kerry gently. 'But I'd like you to try talking to them. The petition gives you a good excuse, doesn't it?'

Sammi swallowed. He still felt really scared. He sat silently for a bit, but Kerry just waited patiently. 'My English is not good for this,' he said at last.

'You might be surprised,' said Kerry. 'Maybe you're better at communicating than you think. You soon understood what Dusty was trying to say, didn't you? We all thought he was just a grumpy donkey, but he's been lovely and gentle with you.'

Sammi thought about it. It wasn't easy to grasp all the words that Kerry was using, but he had worked out what she meant, more or less. What she said about Dusty was true.

He smiled hesitantly. 'I'll try,' he said at last.

'That's all any of us can do,' said Kerry. 'Just do your best.'

His mum was busy cooking when he got home. He knew she found it hard to find exactly the same ingredients that she was used to using back in Afghanistan, but she still managed to create the delicious rice dishes they'd always eaten.

He gave Giti a big hug and grinned as she showed him the homework exercises she'd already finished, then sat down on a stool while his mum stirred something in a saucepan.

'So how's it going on the farm?' his mum asked. 'Did you have a good day today?'

'I really like it there,' said Sammi. 'Most of the animals at City Farm look different to the ones back home, especially the sheep and goats. But the donkey's just the same. He loved the carrots.' Sammi paused. It was such a relief to talk in Pashtun after struggling in English all day! 'His name's Dusty,' he carried on. 'Nobody understood why he was so noisy until I explained to them.'

'I'm not surprised. I haven't seen any other donkeys in England,' said his mum. 'They're not used to them at all.'

'No. Dusty's the only donkey I've seen too,' said Sammi. 'But they care for him really well. He eats lots of hay, and he doesn't have to work very hard. There's nothing to carry or pull, and I don't think they ride him much at all.'

'And you're spoiling him with carrots,' said his mum.

'Well – only a few!' laughed Sammi. 'But actually he might not have a home at all, soon. There are people who want to close the farm down. Everyone's really worried about it.'

Sammi's mum frowned. 'Close it down? Why?'

'They want to build houses there instead. But, Mum, I want the farm to stay open! I feel really happy there and I don't know what'll happen to Dusty if it closes. And it's really bad for Rory too. He's the man you met, the one with the white hair. He lives there, so he'll lose his home.'

'But this isn't Afghanistan!' exclaimed his mum. 'Isn't there anything they can do about it?'

Sammi hesitated, thinking of the petition sitting in his bag. 'Well … they're going to try. They want me to help. They've given me this piece of paper for neighbours to sign, saying they're against it. I'm supposed to go round and ask them to give support.'

'What's this? Show me,' said his mum.

Reluctantly, Sammi got up and fetched the petition.

He translated the declaration at the top of it, missing out the big words that he didn't understand. Half of him hoped that his mum wouldn't approve, but there was no chance of that.

'What a good idea!' she exclaimed. 'You will have to go and talk to people around here! That will be very good for your English!'

Sammi sighed. 'That's what Kerry said.'

'I told you. I like that woman,' said his mum approvingly. 'She's very sensible, and she knows exactly what's good for you. You should do what she says.'

'You really think I can do it?' asked Sammi.

'You? You can do anything you want to do,' said his mum fondly. 'You always did, back home.' She glanced down at his little sister. 'And Giti can help you too.'

Sammi took a deep breath. 'All right then. We'll try. It would be brilliant if I could help City Farm – and Dusty!'

On Monday morning, it felt strange to be sitting back in class. So much had happened since he'd started going to City Farm, and Sammi realized he was a bit more confident now. He still couldn't understand everything Miss Crawley said, but he was getting there.

Jack was at his usual desk. He looked across at Sammi, and they nodded at each other. They weren't exactly what you'd call friends – they didn't spend any time together at break time, or lunch time, as Jack was off with his own friends and Sammi ate alone as usual. Sammi didn't mind. At least Jack didn't seem angry with him any more. All the same, when Jack sidled up to him at the end of the day, he felt quite surprised.

'You going to City Farm?' Jack asked, as they walked out of the gates.

'Yes. I go see Dusty,' said Sammi.

Jack shoved his hands into his pockets. 'D'you want to go together then?' he asked, a bit awkwardly. 'I'm going there too.'

Sammi tried not to show his shock. He started to shrug, then stopped himself. 'OK,' he said instead. 'Thanks, Jack. Good idea.'

Jack gave a lop-sided grin. They walked along to the bus stop and ran to catch the bus, then sat down at the back. They sat saying nothing for a while. Jack looked out of the window at all the houses and offices, but he seemed on edge. Sammi got the idea that he was building up to saying something, so he waited, wondering what it was.

Suddenly, Jack turned to him. 'Listen,' he said, 'I'm sorry I left you. You know, on the farm.'

'Left me?' Sammi was baffled. What did that mean? *Left* was the opposite of *right*…

'Yeah. After the rabbits and all that. I left you on your own.'

Oh. Sammi understood. It was another funny English phrase. He didn't know why Jack was apologizing. It had seemed like quite a normal thing to do. Jack had done his best to show him everything about the rabbits and the guinea pigs, hadn't he? It wasn't Jack's fault that he hadn't been interested. 'Is fine,' he said. He flushed. 'I sorry I call you stupid, in the class. I use wrong word. Not what I mean say.'

Jack shrugged. 'Oh, that's OK. I know it's hard, not being good at English. I'm no good at it, either.'

Sammi was puzzled. 'How? You are English. You know English.'

'Yeah. I can speak it all right,' said Jack. 'But I'm rubbish at reading and writing. That's why we're in the same class.'

Sammi shook his head. 'I not understand.'

 78

Jack took a deep breath. 'I've got a problem,' he explained. 'It's called dys-lex-ia. It means I can understand everything OK, but when I read or write, I get my letters muddled up. Especially "b"s and "d"s, letters that look similar.'

Sammi was listening carefully, but he still couldn't quite get it. Jack dived into his school bag, and pulled out three story books. He handed them to Sammi.

'See here,' he said, pointing to a word on one of the covers. 'I know that says "bad", but if I lose concentration, it looks like "dab".'

It was beginning to make sense. 'I see,' said Sammi. He handed the books back. 'I think this not easy for you. Very hard to learn.'

'Yeah, it's a pain. But I'm getting there,' said Jack. 'It can't be as hard as what you're doing. You've had to learn a new alphabet and everything!' He hesitated, then shoved the books towards Sammi. 'Take them. I brought them into school for you.'

'For me?'

'Yeah. They're easy to read, but not babyish. I thought they might help you.'

Now Sammi was amazed. It was a really nice thing to do. He didn't know what to say. 'Thank you,' he stammered eventually.

'That's OK,' said Jack. 'Don't give up. You're doing really well. You just need practice, that's all!'

Sammi grinned. 'Practice more easy, when I have friends.'

Chapter Eight

'Come on, Sammi! Let's go!' cried Giti.

'Wait, Giti. I have to finish my homework first,' Sammi told her. He had lots of English spellings to learn, and they were giving him a headache.

'Finish it. Finish it,' Giti ordered him, in English, and he laughed.

It was Wednesday evening and Giti had been bouncing around with excitement ever since Sammi had got home from school. They were going to show the petition to all their neighbours, and she couldn't wait to start. Not for the first time, Sammi envied his little sister. For her, it was just a fun adventure with her big brother. She loved chattering away to people and showing off how much she'd learned. It was going to be so much harder for him!

He completed the last few words – *talk, laugh* and *enough* – and checked them against his list of correct spellings. They were all right! He punched the air in triumph. 'I did it!' he yelled.

'So we can go?' begged Giti, hopping from one foot to the other.

'Yes, we can go,' Sammi sighed.

He put his schoolwork away and went to fetch the petition. There were butterflies fluttering in his stomach as they stepped outside and walked up to their next-door neighbour's house. Giti gripped his hand tightly as he rang the doorbell, her eyes shining in anticipation. He smiled down at her, trying not to let her see how nervous he was feeling.

They heard footsteps, and then the door opened. A kind-looking Asian woman peered out. 'Yes? Hello? Who is it?' she asked.

'Hello. I … I am your neighbour. My name is Sammi. And this my sister Giti.'

The door opened a little bit wider. 'Ah … ah. Yes. I saw you move in a few months ago.'

'Yes. We are from Afghanistan.' Sammi cleared his throat.

'Are you? Our family is from Pakistan originally. Neighbours over there as well as over here, then!'

 82

Sammi didn't quite follow, but he heard the word 'neighbour', so he smiled, and nodded.

'Your little sister is very pretty. Aren't you?' said the woman to Giti. 'What did you say your name was?'

'Giti,' said Giti, suddenly all shy.

'And how old are you, Giti?'

'Six,' she said, sounding a little braver. 'But I'm seven very soon.'

'Well, that's very clever, knowing your age in English,' said the woman. 'Do you know what comes after seven?'

'Seven-six-nine-eight-ten!' said Giti, in a rush.

Sammi grinned, then decided he ought to get to the petition. 'We have something we want to show you,' he told the woman. 'Have you ever go City Farm?'

'City Farm? Oh yes. I went there a couple of years ago,' said the woman. 'It's a lovely place. They have wonderful animals, and they make very tasty jam.'

Sammi thrust the petition into her hands. 'Well, you see, they are a problem,' he said. 'The council want City Farm to close. We want to say no, not close it.'

'Close it? But that's not good, not good at all.' The lady looked really upset. 'City Farm has been there for many years. That old barn is a real piece of history.

My own children used to visit when they were younger – they loved it!'

'Then maybe you sign?' asked Sammi, pointing to the place on the form. 'And maybe you come October twelve? Big meeting then. We want many people come, tell council to make City Farm stay open.' He knew he was jumbling his words a little bit, but the woman seemed to understand him perfectly well.

'Of course I'll sign,' said the woman. 'And I'll come on the twelfth as well. It would be a pleasure, a real pleasure. Just wait a minute, I'll go and get a pen.'

'I have a pen,' said Sammi. 'Here!'

As he handed the pen over, he was glowing inside. This was much easier than he'd expected! The woman was really friendly, and now he had his first signature too!

He and Giti carried on along the street. After a few houses, it got easier and easier to describe what was happening up at City Farm. Sammi even managed to explain that all the animals would be made homeless if the farm closed down. A couple of people shook their heads when they saw Sammi on the doorstep with his petition, and shut the door before he had chance to say anything, but most people wanted to understand exactly what was going on, so they were happy to listen to him, and help when he stumbled over his words.

They reached the end of the street and knocked at the final door. This time it was a boy who answered. He looked a couple of years older than Sammi and had a football tucked under his arm.

'Hi,' began Sammi. 'My name is Sammi. I live close to you...' He waved with his hand down the street.

The boy looked interested at once. 'Cool,' he said. 'Do you play football?'

Sammi was surprised. 'Yes,' he said. 'Of course!'

'Thing is, we're looking for more people to play,' the boy told him. 'We go down the sports centre every Wednesday night, but a few people have given up recently so we're a bit short on numbers.'

Sammi frowned, trying to follow. 'You want to play football… ?' he asked, worried in case he'd got it wrong. He hesitated. 'With me? Now?'

The boy grinned, and glanced at Giti. 'Well, maybe next time,' he said. 'You any good? What position do you play?'

Sammi knew all the footballer positions from watching television. 'Midfield,' he said. 'Thank you. I would like to play. But today I very busy.' He waved the petition. 'We are trying to help City Farm. The council want it close, but we all say no.'

'City Farm! We went there once with school. I remember collecting eggs from the chicken sheds. It was cool.'

'Then you sign?' asked Sammi.

'Let's see,' said the boy.

Sammi handed him the sheet, and the boy read it over quickly. 'Sure I'll sign it,' he said. 'My mum and dad will too. And my nan – she's visiting today. Hang on, I'll just take it in to them.'

The boy disappeared into the house, and came back a few moments later with three new signatures on the petition. Then, with Sammi watching, he wrote down his own name too. *Robin Stewart*, Sammi read.

'Also we need people to come to the farm on October twelve,' Sammi told him. 'You can come, and bring other players?'

'Why not?' grinned Robin. 'Sure, we'll be there. It would be fun to see City Farm again.'

'Thank you, Robin,' said Sammi. 'See you soon!'

'Yeah, sure,' said Robin, as Sammi and Giti retreated down the path. 'And don't forget – football in the sports centre next Wednesday, six o'clock! I'll be counting on you!'

'OK,' called Sammi happily over his shoulder.

As they walked off down the road again, Sammi was beaming. He'd made a new friend, just like that! He couldn't think of anything better than having a local football team to play with. Kerry and his mum had been so right. If he hadn't been brave, trying to get names on the petition, he wouldn't have met Robin and he wouldn't be spending so much time chatting away in English. Maybe he could build a happy life here, after all … and it was all thanks to City Farm.

Chapter Nine

'Dusty!' Sammi leaned over the gate, calling his friend.

The donkey raised his head and immediately brayed a greeting. With the head collar slung over his shoulder, Sammi let himself into the paddock. Dusty trotted towards him through the grass, which was still sparkling with dew – it was early on Saturday 11 October, and Sammi wanted to make the most of every minute he had left on City Farm.

Dusty nosed Sammi's pockets for carrots, as usual. 'Just one,' said Sammi, fishing one out. 'You can have more once we've had some fun!'

While Dusty chewed up the carrot, Sammi slipped the head collar over his head. Then, still holding the lead rope, he vaulted onto the donkey's back.

'Come on, Dusty, let's go!' he said, giving the

donkey's sides a little kick with his heels.

Dusty seemed puzzled for a minute, so Sammi nudged him again. 'Come on, Dusty,' he whispered.

Suddenly, with a snort, Dusty leaped into life. He trotted across the paddock, around the old oak tree and back towards the gate. Sammi grinned from ear to ear. This was exactly what he and his cousin used to do in Afghanistan!

With another nudge of his heels, Dusty broke into a canter. 'That's it! That's it!' yelled Sammi. 'Faster, Dusty!'

Dusty was getting very excited now. He tore around the field, making Stanley and Swift look up from grazing to stare. Stanley whinnied loudly. He was clearly surprised at his friend's strange behaviour! With his tail held high, he came and trotted alongside for a few strides, before getting bored and going back to his grass.

Around they went again. Out of the corner of his eye, Sammi saw Asha appear at the gate, so he gave a little tug on the lead rope to slow the donkey down. 'That's enough, Dusty!' he called. 'Whoa, boy!'

Dusty charged up to the gate, then stopped dead. In fact, he stopped so suddenly that Sammi slid forward down his shoulder and landed with a bump on the grass.

'Sammi!' exclaimed Asha. 'Are you OK?'

Sammi was laughing so hard he could hardly catch his breath. He managed to nod, and felt Dusty nuzzling his hair with his rubbery lips. 'I … fine,' he said eventually. 'This grass very soft!' He struggled to his feet and threw his arms around Dusty's neck. 'This very good, Dusty, no? We have much fun.'

Asha was looking a little bit shocked. 'I've never seen anything quite like that!' she said. 'You were going so fast, and you don't even have a saddle!'

'I not need saddle,' said Sammi. 'This how I ride in Afghanistan. You want try?'

'Oh! No, thank you,' said Asha quickly. She grinned. 'I'm glad you've both been enjoying yourselves so much though! It did look exciting.'

Dusty seemed to agree, because he stretched out his neck and started to bray. 'Ee-yore, ee-yore!' he went.

'That enough now, Dusty,' Sammi told him. 'Come on. You be good for Asha.'

He stroked Dusty's neck, and the donkey quietened down. Then he nuzzled Sammi's pockets.

'He remember!' laughed Sammi. 'I promise him carrot after we ride.'

'You know, he's so different now,' said Asha. 'He's so happy, like a completely different donkey! It would

 90

be so unfair if he has to leave. If *anyone* has to leave! Oh, Sammi – I really, really hope our petition works. I've worked so hard this week, trying to get signatures. Did you get some as well?'

'Of course,' said Sammi. 'Come, I show you. Petition in feed room, in my bag.'

He unclipped the head collar and gave Dusty a pat. 'I come back later,' he promised the donkey.

Together, he and Asha walked up to the yard. Sammi found his petition and they counted the names on it.

'...forty-one … forty-two … forty-three!' Sammi finished, in English.

Forty-three names, all collected by him and Giti. He stared at the sheet. He could hardly believe what he'd managed to do. He felt very proud of himself, but at the same time, he was worried. The petition had to work. It just *had* to!

Asha looked at his sheet in admiration. 'You did so well, Sammi!'

Sammi smiled at her. He knew that Asha would have collected loads more names than him, but that was hardly surprising, she was so friendly!

'Come on, let's go and show Kerry,' said Asha.

'OK,' said Sammi, and they hurried up to the barn.

 91

Inside, even though it was still so early, the whole place was in turmoil. Kerry had started packing away her most important paperwork, just in case they had to move everything out. Rory had packed up many of his belongings in the farmhouse, and some of his boxes were now piled up in the barn. Sammi stared at the scene, a lump rising in his throat. He couldn't believe that this really might be the end for City Farm.

'Ah, you two! There you are!' called Kerry. 'I'm just counting the names on the petitions. I think we've done pretty well … let me see yours…'

Asha and Sammi added their sheets to the pile that Kerry had in front of her, just as Rory came in through the big wooden door carrying a heavy box. He dumped it down as Kerry flicked through the petition sheets.

'Wow! You two have done us proud!' exclaimed Kerry. 'I think this will take our total to over five hundred signatures!'

Asha jumped up and down in excitement. 'Five hundred! That's loads! They *can't* close us down!'

But Sammi was watching Kerry and Rory. They didn't look quite so excited. He could see they wanted to believe the petition would work, but they didn't dare. He took in the boxes piled everywhere, and the

 92

stacks of papers on Kerry's desk. He knew all about packing. When you were about to leave a place you loved, you couldn't bear to move all the things that made your life so special. You didn't do it unless you thought you really, really had to.

'Let's wait and see, Asha,' said Kerry. 'It's good to know that we have all this support. That feels nice, even if...' Her voice trailed off, and she sighed.

'But I know so many people are coming tomorrow!' said Asha. 'They're all going to tell the council what they think! There'll be hundreds of people here...'

'That's great, Asha,' said Kerry. Her voice was oddly flat. 'But the truth is, we have to be ready to close down. That means packing things away, and saying goodbye to the animals. You know we've had to make arrangements for them all to go somewhere else.'

Asha's face fell, and there was a brief silence. Sammi knew that Kerry had worked incredibly hard over the last week. She'd spent hours on the phone, ringing rescue homes and farms and even pet shops, trying to find good homes for all the animals.

'Aye,' said Rory. 'I wish I believed this petition would work. But I've known Derrick Jarvis for a good few years. He likes to get his papers in order. If he says we're closing, then … we probably are.' He looked as though he was carrying a big heavy sack of sorrow on his shoulders.

'Rory,' asked Sammi. 'Where will you go? City Farm your home. You have somewhere to sleep?'

'Bless you, lad,' said Rory. 'Don't you worry about me. I have a brother up north, with a farm. I'll be going to stay with him.'

Sammi was glad. He couldn't bear the thought of Rory being homeless. But he felt terribly sad too, because he might not be seeing him any more. Or Kerry, or any of the friendly staff in the City Farm cafe. Worst of all, he wouldn't be able to see Dusty…

Sammi joined Rory and Jack in the farmhouse, helping them to pack Rory's belongings, then shift boxes to the barn. They worked at it all morning, only stopping for a quick sandwich. Then Kerry asked Sammi and Asha to take down all the lovely children's pictures that lined the walls of the barn. Asha made sure they packed them really neatly, so that they wouldn't be damaged.

'You never know – we might be able to put them back up again, if the petition works!' she said.

'I hope you right,' agreed Sammi.

 94

When at last they'd finished, Sammi went out back out to the paddock. He approached slowly this time, looking at Stanley, Swift and Dusty as they munched their way across the grass. Dusty had calmed down from his early-morning adventure, and was grazing alongside Stanley and Swift. They had no idea what was about to happen to them, he thought sadly.

'Dusty!' he called, stepping up to the fence.

The donkey looked pleased to see Sammi again. 'Eeee-yore, eeee-yore!' he squealed, then trotted over to the gate.

Sammi stroked his long, furry face. 'I'm going to miss you,' he told him. 'You're the first friend I made here at City Farm. You've helped me a lot, did you know that?'

Dusty butted Sammi's arm, then started to nibble at his sleeve.

'Hey!' laughed Sammi. 'I know we're friends, but you're not supposed to eat me.' He fished in his pocket and found half a carrot – the last one. 'Here you are.'

Dusty crunched it up, then stood quietly, resting his head on Sammi's arm.

'I haven't known you very long, but I think we understand each other pretty well, don't we?' Sammi carried on. He felt a bit silly, talking to a donkey. But then Dusty snorted through his nostrils and butted him gently again, as though he'd understood every word.

'Sammi!' called Asha's voice. She ran around the side of the feed rooms and along to the field gate. 'I've come to say goodbye to Stanley and Swift and Dusty. Then I want to go and see Curly and Lizzie, then all the goats – and then I have to spend lots of time with Bubble and Squeak because they're my favourites…' She leaned over the gate and patted Dusty's neck. 'I so wish we had longer with them all,' she said wistfully. 'I don't know what I'm going to do with myself if I don't have City Farm to come to!'

Sammi nodded. He hadn't been coming to City Farm anywhere near as long as Asha, but it had already made such a difference to him. He looked around, thinking that there would soon be big houses sitting right here, where the sunshine was beaming down through the trees and lighting up Dusty's coat … It was an awful thought. He couldn't bear to imagine it.

'Let's go and see the other animals together,' suggested Asha.

The afternoon sun seemed to give everything a golden glow as they wandered around the farm. Curly and Lizzie ran over, bleating, as they reached their paddock, and the goats gave them a noisy welcome too.

'They all think it's feeding time!' said Asha. 'I wish we could explain to them exactly what's happening. It's not fair, it's really not!'

They scratched heads and patted necks and made a fuss of everyone, then moved on to say goodbye to Cynthia, the Tamworth pig. They were just approaching her sty when they heard Kerry's voice floating from the direction of the barn. 'Asha! Sammi! Where are you?'

'Coming!' they called.

Kerry was standing in the barn doorway holding a big tray of cakes from the cafe. 'We have a very useful job for everyone,' she explained. 'We don't want these cakes to go to waste. We need to finish them off today, so we're going to gather everyone in the pony paddock to have a picnic.'

'Oh! That's a wonderful idea! I love picnics!' said Asha. She hesitated. 'But I haven't said a proper goodbye to the rabbits and guinea pigs yet. Do you think they could join us, somehow?'

'Well, as this might be our last full day, I think we should include as many of the animals as possible,' said Kerry. 'I've already asked Rory and Jack to sort out some mini pens for the smaller animals. The others can all just join in for once!'

'Brilliant,' enthused Asha. 'Sammi and I can go around telling everyone what's happening! And can we get treats together for all the animals to eat as well?'

'Yes, of course,' said Kerry. 'That would be really helpful.'

'We'll get started then,' said Asha. 'Is that OK with you, Sammi?'

But Sammi had no idea what they were talking about. He was feeling completely lost. 'I don't know,' he said. 'What is *peekinick*?'

Chapter Ten

Asha clapped her hand to her forehead. 'Oh, Sammi, I'm sorry!' she exclaimed. 'Of course you don't know what a picnic is. It's when we get food from inside and take it outside somewhere lovely – like a beach at the seaside, or the middle of a wood, or the pony paddock! Then we all sit around on the ground to eat it.'

'Oh.' Sammi was puzzled. Asha seemed really excited, but he couldn't understand what all the fuss was about. It was quite normal to eat outside, sitting on the ground – they used to do it in Afghanistan all the time.

'Come on. It'll be lovely,' Asha carried on. 'Let's go and tell Cynthia first – we were going there anyway! And we'll sort out some treats for her to eat.'

'What is treats?' asked Sammi.

'Treats are the favourite naughty things that everyone loves to eat,' explained Asha. 'They're the things that you're not allowed to have too often!'

'We have treats too, at this *peekinick*?'

'Oh, yes, lots,' said Asha. 'Didn't you see all those cakes that Kerry was holding?'

Sammi was beginning to like the sound of this. He followed Asha as she skipped off towards the feed room.

'We can take some swedes for Cynthia,' said Asha. 'She loves them! And while we're here, we can collect a bucket of pony nuts for Dusty and the horses. Perhaps you could do that while I get the swedes?'

Sammi went over to the sacks of feed and shovelled a couple of scoops of tasty-looking brown pony nuts into one of the buckets. He popped a few in his pocket too, just in case. He'd never seen special feed like that before coming to the UK, and he couldn't imagine that they tasted very nice. But then he'd seen the donkey tuck in, and it was clear that Dusty adored them!

They headed towards Cynthia's pen with Asha chattering all the way. 'We can take Cynthia down to the paddock,' she said. 'She'll follow anyone who's carrying something tasty. If we're not careful she'll try to eat all the pony nuts too – and our sandwiches and all the cakes!'

Sammi laughed at the thought of the pig trying to steal everyone's food. They arrived at her pen. Cynthia caught one whiff of the swedes and she was at her gate in no time, snuffling and grunting.

'Come on then, Cynthia!' laughed Asha. 'Follow us!'

It was really funny, watching the fat orange pig trotting after them down the yard. Inside the paddock, they placed the swedes in one corner. Cynthia grunted in excitement and started to gobble them up.

'Those swedes won't last long!' laughed Rory. He and Jack were busy with bits of wood and netting, so Asha and Sammi went to take a look.

'We've already fixed some netting around some posts here,' said Jack. 'D'you and Sammi want to go and get the rabbits and guinea pigs?'

'We'd love to!' beamed Asha. 'Let's go, Sammi!'

As they headed out of the field, Bea appeared with a big tray of sandwiches. Kerry was just behind her, carrying an old rug.

'Let's lay the rug near the old oak tree,' said Kerry. 'That's the perfect place for a picnic!'

'Oooh! We're nearly ready,' exclaimed Asha. 'We'd

better hurry up, Sammi, or there won't be any treats left!'

'Don't worry,' laughed Kerry. 'There's plenty to go round. And we won't start without you!'

Asha and Sammi rushed off towards the rabbit and guinea pig runs. Asha picked up Custard and handed her to Sammi. 'Can you take her?' she asked. 'We'll have to do shifts to get them all there one by one!'

Sammi was surprised at how heavy the rabbit was. She stayed quiet in his arms as he hurried back to the paddock, and put her down in her special picnic pen. Custard started nibbling at the lovely lush grass straight away. Then Asha arrived with Crumble. By the time they'd fetched the two other rabbits and the two guinea pigs, Rory and Jack had fetched the goats and sheep to join the picnic, while Bea and the other cafe workers had added lots of cakes to all the yummy sandwiches.

'Come and sit down, Sammi!' called Kerry, who had settled down on one corner of the rug.

Sammi sat down next to her and crossed his legs, just like he used to do in Afghanistan. This picnic was making him feel quite at home.

Then Rory appeared from the barn with big jugs of home-made lemonade. 'We used to drink gallons

 102

of this when I was a lad,' he said. 'As far as I'm concerned, you can't have a picnic without it!'

All the bustle and all the different animals made Dusty, Stanley and Swift very curious. They stopped grazing and came over, their ears pricked forward. Asha and Sammi tipped the pony nuts onto the grass, so that all three of them could have some.

As soon as there were none left, Dusty started to bray loudly, and Kerry put her hands over her ears.

'Sammi! Can you make him stop?' she asked.

'I think so,' grinned Sammi. He got up and went to Dusty's side, then delved into his pocket. 'I keep a few pony nut here.'

Dusty was very happy to see the nuts, and munched them in double-quick time. Sammi went back to sit on the rug, and Dusty followed him, gazing hopefully at the picnic.

'I think he want cake,' said Sammi.

'Hmm, yes, I'm sure he does,' said Kerry. 'But I think pony nuts are quite enough!'

They all began to tuck into the mountains of food from the cafe. As they did so, a little stripy furry creature appeared – Silky the cat! She made her way around everyone, rubbing herself against their legs and purring.

'Oh! We haven't got a treat for Silky,' said Asha.

'Don't worry about that,' said Bea. 'One of the cream cakes tipped off a tray near the barn, and guess who licked up the cream?'

'That's all right then!' giggled Asha. 'We wouldn't want you to miss out, Silky!'

Rory reached for a big slice of pork pie. 'Ah, this takes me back,' he said, after munching a big bite. 'I remember the early days, when we first opened the farm to visitors. It was a glorious summer, hardly rained at all! And there was old Mrs Davies who used to make chutney to go with the pies. Delicious, it was – we used to sell pots and pots of it.'

'I remember that chutney,' agreed Kerry. 'She was famous for it! Such a pity she moved away.'

Just then, Stanley the pony came over and butted Kerry with his soft nose. 'Hello, Stanley!' she greeted him. 'I expect you remember your first days here too, don't you?' She began to explain to everyone what happened. 'He was really lonely because his owner had died, and he'd been left on his own in his field,' she said. 'He was on his own here too, when he first came to us, and he hated it every time I left him – he'd call and call until I was out of sight. So I decided to come and eat my sandwiches with him at lunch time, to keep him happy.'

'That must have been before Dusty arrived then,' said Jack.

'Oh yes, it was,' said Kerry. 'Dusty made a big difference to him. He might have seemed grumpy to us, but Stanley didn't mind. They soon became great friends!'

Sammi listened, then smiled. 'You see,' he said to everyone. 'Dusty always useful. He help Stanley, and he help me.'

Kerry laughed. 'That's true, Sammi! And I'm sure that with you next to him, he could become even more useful – he could start giving children donkey rides!'

'I like that,' declared Sammi. 'Yes, I think that very good idea.'

'I think you're forgetting something,' said Rory quietly.

The picnic suddenly fell silent. Of course. Dusty might never get a chance to be so useful. This might be City Farm's last day. Sammi felt a wave of sadness. Asha put her slice of cake back down on her plate, and looked glum. Jack frowned, and laid his head on his knees.

'Now, come on, everyone,' said Bea brightly. 'This won't do. Let's take it a day at a time. Who knows what will happen? We're having a lovely picnic and there are still some delicious cream cakes waiting to be eaten.'

'Well said, Bea!' said Kerry. 'You can pass me one of those cakes, please!'

They were all so busy chatting and eating that they didn't notice what was happening behind Rory's back. It was Sammi who noticed first.

'Rory!' he exclaimed. 'See – the goats!'

The greedy goats had spotted the cakes, just to the edge of the rug. And they were all gathered around it, tucking in!

'Hey!' yelled Rory, scrambling to his feet. 'They're not for you! You've had your treats. Shoo, shoo!'

The goats snatched what they could before running off under the trees to join Curly and Lizzie, who were being much better behaved, happily eating grass.

Rory sat down again, shaking his head. 'Goats. You need eyes in the back of your head with them, you really do.'

'I think all goats same,' said Sammi. 'In Afghanistan, they like eat everything too.'

'Did they get many of those pastries?' asked Bea. 'Cheeky things. I spent ages making them!'

'There's a few they haven't touched,' said Rory.

'Not many though!'

'Never mind. I don't know about everyone else, but I'm full,' said Kerry. 'I don't think I could eat another thing!'

Sammi had to agree. He'd eaten a mound of sandwiches and three big slices of cake, all washed down with Rory's delicious lemonade.

The warm autumn day was drawing to a close, the old oak and horse chestnut trees in the paddock casting long shadows over the grass. As the others began to pack away the picnic, he wasn't sure he could move! And he certainly didn't want to. Life at City Farm was so special. He looked around at all the faces that had welcomed him – especially Jack, Asha and Dusty. In a short space of time, he had become part of this little community. At last, he felt like he belonged.

Chapter Eleven

That evening, Sammi sat down with the books that Jack had given him. He had already finished one of them, and he was over halfway through a second one. Jack was right – they were quite easy to read, but the stories weren't too boring. In fact, they were exciting adventures that made him want to carry on, and he found he was whizzing through the pages. If he finished this one tonight, he'd be able to return it to Jack in the morning.

His mum came to sit next to him. 'Are these books from school?' she asked him.

Sammi looked up. 'Not really,' he said. 'They're from Jack. He's in my class at school, but we weren't friends until we met at City Farm.'

'City Farm, City Farm!' smiled his mum. 'That's

 108

all you want to talk about these days. Well, I'm very happy. And I have something to tell you.'

'What kind of thing?'

'Our neighbour came round today,' said his mum. 'The woman from Pakistan. I couldn't understand everything she said, but I worked out that she's going to City Farm tomorrow. She suggested we go there together. What do you think?'

'Mum! That's a great idea,' said Sammi. 'She speaks really good English. You'll learn a lot from her!'

'Yes. Maybe she'll become a friend. That would be good for me, I think.'

Sammi grinned at her. Of course his mum needed friends here in England, just as much as he did.

Sunday 12 October dawned at last – the day that everyone was dreading. Sammi got to City Farm early. His mum would be along later with Giti and their neighbour, but he wanted to be there to see Dusty, check on what was happening and see if there was anything he could do to help.

Rory and Jack were already at work, milking the goats as usual. The animals still had to be looked after properly, even if they were going to move from their homes very soon. Sammi watched Jack struggle with the buckets, and jumped forward to help him. Jack grinned at him.

'I finish two books,' Sammi told Jack proudly, as they walked across the yard towards the barn. 'I bring them back for you today.'

'That was quick!' said Jack. 'D'you want some more, afterwards? I don't have any myself but there are loads in the library.'

'The what?' Sammi hadn't heard the word before.

'Li-bra-ry,' said Jack slowly. 'It's where you can borrow books to read. We can go there together sometime, if you like.'

'I would like that,' agreed Sammi. 'Thanks, Jack.'

As they swung open the barn's creaking wooden door, Kerry was standing behind her desk, looking nervous. She was holding a piece of paper and muttering to herself, turning the paper away and then muttering again.

'What's going on, Kerry?' asked Jack.

Kerry gave a big sigh. She ran a hand over her braids, then fiddled with one of the silver beads that dangled from them. 'I'm just practising my speech,' she told them. 'I think it's really important that we explain to everyone what City Farm is all about, and how much it's contributed to our community.'

'A speech! That sounds scary,' said Jack.

'Too right it's scary,' agreed Kerry.

Just then, the barn door burst open again and Asha rushed in.

'Kerry, Derrick Jarvis is here! And he's got a big *CLOSED* sign in his car – I don't know what he's going to do with it …'

'Has he indeed? Right. I'll deal with him. Come on.' Kerry put her speech down and led everyone outside. A group of council workers were gathering in the car park, some with yellow hard hats and fluorescent jackets like the ones who had come before. Derrick Jarvis was there with another man by his side, chatting away with the *CLOSED* sign under his arm.

Kerry marched across the car park in her leopard-print wellies, and went straight up to Derrick Jarvis. 'Good morning, Derrick,' she greeted him.

'Ah, Kerry,' he said. 'I'm just going to get the men to hammer this into place. I hope you've put all your affairs in order – the development people will be here to start work first thing on Monday morning.'

'Our affairs are always in order here at City Farm, Derrick,' Kerry told him calmly. 'But I think you'll find there are a lot of people who want to come and look around for one last time. So it might be better to wait until the end of the day to put that sign up, don't you think?' She nodded towards the main gate. 'You see, there are visitors just arriving.'

Sammi's heart gave a leap. His new footballing friend Robin had walked in – with a big group of boys just behind him!

Derrick Jarvis looked very cross, and harrumphed grumpily. 'If this is another delaying tactic of yours—' he began.

'Not at all,' said Kerry smoothly. 'This has always been a community project, Derrick. So if the community want to come in on our last day, I really don't think we should stop them. And to show just how much support we have, I'd like to show you this—'

She held out the sheaf of petition papers, but Derrick just looked away. Sammi felt shocked. This man was so rude! But more people were arriving all the time – he wouldn't be able to ignore *everyone*, would he? Asha rushed off to greet some friends, then Jack started waving furiously at someone he knew. The big yard at City Farm was starting to fill up!

Kerry tried again. 'I really think you should look at this—'

But Derrick was staring at the crowds coming in. 'This is most irregular,' he muttered. 'We should have that sign up by now.'

Then the man at his side interrupted. 'It's all right, Derrick. The sign can wait,' he said. Then he turned to Kerry. 'I'm Mr Collins, Derrick's boss. I've come to oversee what happens today.'

Kerry shook his hand. 'Good to meet you, Mr Collins,' she said. 'I hope you're fully aware of what a big impact this closure is going to have. I think you'll find that it's not at all popular with local people. In fact…'

Mr Collins coughed. 'Our main concern is to make the best use of the land.'

'Exactly,' said Kerry. 'And when you see the support we have today, I hope you'll begin to realize what the *best use* really is.'

People were continuing to stream in through the gates. Some of them explored the yard or wandered into the garden, while others took a walk around the grounds to see all the animals in the fields and enclosures. After about an hour, Kerry called Sammi, Jack, and Asha over to the barn.

'I'd like you to go and gather all the visitors together,' she told them. 'Bring everyone back here, to the front of the barn. It's time I made a speech. Take a petition

 113

with you, in case anyone hasn't signed it.'

The three of them ran off in different directions to do as she said. To his delight, Sammi saw his mum, Giti and the neighbour coming through the gates, and he directed them to the right place. Then he rushed off to the paddocks to fetch anyone who might still be out there. He found Robin and his friends, and ushered them back to the yard. When they arrived, he stared in amazement. The yard was completely packed!

He left Robin and elbowed his way to stand near Jack, Rory and Asha. Kerry was looking more nervous than ever, but she stood up on a wooden bench and began to speak.

'Welcome to City Farm,' she said. 'And thank you so much for coming.' Her voice was a little bit wobbly at first, but it got stronger as she carried on. 'I think you'll all agree that there's nowhere quite like City Farm. Where else can children come and see goats, chickens, pigs and donkeys in a city environment? And not just children – I know that many adults have enjoyed coming here over the years.'

A murmur of agreement rippled through the crowd. 'What's more, this is more than just a farm. The Harvest Hope project was set up for children

 114

facing a difficult period in their lives. Here, they've found new purpose and happiness through looking after other creatures, and a new sense of community too. I'm happy to say that we've helped many to find their way.'

Sammi found himself nodding. He couldn't agree more. But now, Kerry's voice was sounding more and more sad. 'So today is a tragic day for me. Members of our own council are here with us, and they're here not to support us, but to close us down. Ladies and gentlemen, if you have signed our petition, I'm very grateful...' She turned to Rory, who was standing by her side. 'How many signatures do we have, Rory?'

'Five hundred and seventy-four,' he told her.

'Five hundred and seventy-four members of this community have signed, saying that they wish the farm to remain open. But sadly, the council doesn't want to hear. Five hundred and seventy-four people say no to closure. The council still says yes.'

The muttering among the crowd now sounded indignant. Someone shouted out, 'Shame!'

'So, unfortunately, City Farm has to say goodbye to you all. Thank you again for coming. I value your support more than I can say.'

Kerry stopped, looking upset. She stepped down,

 115

and there was a smattering of applause. With a flourish, Rory handed the pile of petition sheets to Mr Collins. He looked embarrassed, and flicked through them hastily. Derrick Jarvis said something into his ear, and he nodded, then turned his back to Rory and Kerry and began to walk away.

Out of the corner of his eye, Sammi spied one of the council workers with the *CLOSED* sign in one hand, and a hammer in the other. Surely that couldn't be it? After everything that Kerry had said, and all the names on the petition, they were just going to carry on and shut City Farm? Could Derrick Jarvis and Mr Collins ignore them all, just like that?

Suddenly, he knew what he had to do. Feeling very nervous, he stepped forward, past Asha and Jack, and forced himself up onto the bench. Kerry stared at him in surprise. 'Sammi, what are you… ?'

He stared down at her, his cheeks burning. But then he saw his mum's face in the crowd and opened his mouth. Somehow, he began to speak.

'I come to Harvest Hope project…' he began. His voice was quiet, and he realized that no one could hear him. He cleared his throat.

'I come to Harvest Hope project three weeks ago,' he tried again, louder this time, and some of the crowd noticed. They nudged their neighbours, and the chatter slowly died down as people turned his way.

Sammi searched his heart for what he wanted to say. 'I never think England can be my home,' he said. 'I miss Afghanistan. I miss my family. I miss everyone.' He looked for his mum's face again, and saw her eyes wide with amazement. She nodded at him, urging him to carry on.

'But here at City Farm, I make friends. For first time, I make friends. I make friends with animals and I make friends with people. Now I think...' He paused, struggling for the right words. 'Now I think that maybe I can be home in England after all.'

He came to a halt. Everyone was silent. He glanced down at Kerry, and saw that she had tears in her eyes.

'Thank you, Sammi,' she whispered, as he stepped down.

The crowd had started to applaud when Asha leaped up onto the bench and began to speak. 'Sammi's so right!' she told everyone. 'I'm on the Harvest Hope project too, and it's helped me so much! I was sick in hospital with leukaemia for months. But then when I started to get better I came here, and it's made me so much stronger! I love working with all the animals and looking after them and learning about them, and

Kerry and Rory are so supportive and you just know when you're here on City Farm that anything and everything is possible after all!'

She paused to draw breath, and now the crowd had started clapping loudly, and cheering their support.

'I think the best part was when I first started feeding the guinea pigs, and then they started recognizing me whenever I came near and making their crazy squeaking sound,' Asha carried on. 'Or maybe it was when I took some feed to the goats and they nearly knocked me over, they were so excited! I realized I'd have to get strong and fit if I was going to deal with *them*.'

Everyone laughed, then cheered again. As Asha kept on with her string of stories, Sammi noticed that Jack was lining up to speak, along with a row of other children that he didn't recognize. Kerry must have seen him looking because she whispered to him. 'They've all been on the Harvest Hope project, like you,' she told him. 'There's Emily, Laura, Katie and Darren. Oh, and Zoe too.'

Asha was coming to the end of another funny story. With everyone laughing, Rory persuaded her that she'd got her message across.

'Come on, lass, let the others speak now,' Sammi

 118

heard him say.

Jack took her place, and sounded a bit nervous. He told everyone how he'd grown up on a farm and had really missed it when he moved to the city.

'I love City Farm,' he said simply. 'I don't know what I'm going to do without it.'

He clambered down, his cheeks a bit pink, so that Emily, Laura, Katie, Darren and Zoe could say their bit. As they spoke, Sammi suddenly realized something else. His English had improved so much in the last few weeks that he understood everything they said. Maybe, after all, it wouldn't always be a struggle. One day, he'd be able to chatter away in English just like he could in Pashtun.

The crowd was loving every minute of it, but Sammi was beginning to get anxious. It was all very well having their support, but what about the council? He couldn't even see Derrick Jarvis any more, or the men in yellow jackets. He wondered what they were up to.

Suddenly, a loud voice boomed over all the others, silencing the crowd. 'Let's stop all this now,' it called. 'I think we've heard quite enough!'

Chapter Twelve

Sammi craned his neck to see who it was. The crowd parted slightly, and he saw the group of council workers, and Mr Collins elbowing his way to the front. He held his breath. *Now* what was going to happen? Everyone muttered and murmured as Mr Collins made his way forward. Sammi felt really nervous. What had he meant, *we've heard quite enough*? Was he just fed up of hearing about the farm and wanted to get on with closing it? Or was it something else?

With a bit of huffing and puffing, Mr Collins stepped up onto the bench. He took a handkerchief out of his pocket and mopped his forehead before beginning to speak.

'As I'm sure you all know, City Farm has been funded by the council for many years,' he said.

'And I'm very proud that we've supported such an wonderful project. It's been very touching to hear all these lovely stories.' He paused. 'But as you know, this land is a valuable asset.'

There was a rumble of protest as everyone guessed what he was about to say. Mr Collins raised his hand for quiet. 'Every now and again, we have to ask ourselves this very important question: are we still making the best use of the council's money and assets?'

Sammi looked round in frustration. Mr Collins' English was so difficult to follow. Why didn't he just get on with it, he wondered, and tell everyone exactly what he was going to do?

'Shame!' cried someone again.

'Wait, wait,' said Mr Collins. 'Please bear with me. Today, I've seen something I never expected to see. I've seen that the whole community values City Farm, and it offers hope and support to our young people.'

'Keep it open, then!' called someone else.

Mr Collins smiled. 'What I've discovered today is that we couldn't be spending our money better,' he said. 'And so the council will continue to fund City Farm for the foreseeable future!'

'HURRAHHH!' shouted Jack, at Sammi's side, and the whole crowd joined in!

Sammi didn't understand everything that Mr Collins had said. 'Is open?' he shouted to Jack. 'Is OK?'

'Yes!' Jack yelled back. Asha began to jump up and down like a yo-yo. Rory's smile was so huge that Sammi thought it might split his face in half! Kerry did a jig in her leopard-print wellies, and everyone in the crowd laughed and cheered at the top of their voices.

Sammi hugged everyone in turn – Rory and Kerry, then Jack and Asha. Then he rushed to find Giti and his mum, and hugged them too. Everyone was so happy!

'Sammi! Come with us!' called Asha, reaching for his hand through the crowd. 'We're going to show all our favourite parts of the farm to Mr Collins!'

Sammi's mum grinned and waved him off to join the little group of people who were clustered around Mr Collins.

'First, I think I should see inside the famous old barn,' said Mr Collins. 'Good lord! This is such a splendid old building. I rather suspect that it will be of historic interest to our heritage department ... Let's go in, shall we?'

Everyone piled through the big old wooden door. Kerry took him into her office to show him the stack of files, recording all the children who had been helped by the Harvest Hope project. Then Asha dug out all the colourful pictures that had been sent in by schools.

They headed outside again with Mr Collins full of enthusiasm. 'I've just had a thought,' he said. 'A colleague's daughter has just had a big operation. It'll take her a long time to fully recover, but I can imagine that the Harvest Hope project would do her the world of good. Would you consider her, do you think?'

'Of course we would,' said Kerry. 'Rehabilitation work is one of the things we do best. Just send me her details and we can start the process. Now, which part of the farm would you like to visit first? The garden, perhaps?'

'Sounds wonderful,' agreed Mr Collins.

Out in the front yard, the council workers were still standing around, wondering what to do. Derrick Jarvis was standing with them, his face furious. The worker holding the *CLOSED* sign stepped forward.

'What should we do with this, Mr Collins?' he asked.

'Well, we won't be needing it here,' said Mr Collins. 'Give it to Mr Jarvis. I'm sure he'll find a use for it somewhere else.'

The worker handed the sign over. Sammi watched

as Mr Jarvis turned on his heel and marched off towards his car. But then, instead of putting the sign in his boot, he held it out in front of him for a second. He shook his head in disgust, and broke the sign over his knee. It split neatly into two pieces!

Grinning to himself, Sammi skipped after the others as they wandered down through the flower beds in the garden. Mr Collins was very impressed with all the vegetables, and particularly loved the pond with all the ducks and geese waddling around it. The swans sat safely on the other side of the water, looking very beautiful and elegant.

'Reminds me of my childhood!' he exclaimed happily. 'I dare say you get plenty of tadpoles in the spring, don't you?'

'Aye,' Rory told him. 'There's frogs and toads – the clumps of frogspawn and the strings of toadspawn. I always love pointing out the difference to littl'uns.'

Sammi gave Asha a nudge. 'What's frog and toad?' he asked.

Asha immediately went down on all fours and did an impression, croaking and hopping along beside the pond. Everyone burst out laughing.

'Asha, what on earth are you doing?' asked Kerry.

  124

'I'm explaining to Sammi,' said Asha. 'He wasn't sure what we were talking about!'

'Is OK,' giggled Sammi. 'I understand now.' There was no mistaking what Asha was imitating!

They walked way round past the chicken coops, with their cosy nest boxes. Jack suggested that Mr Collins have a look for an egg, and sure enough, he found a lovely fresh brown one with speckles at one end.

'We'd better take that up to the barn,' said Kerry. 'Or perhaps you'd like to take it with you?'

'I'd love to take it,' said Mr Collins. 'I'll show it to my daughter. She'll be thrilled to think her old dad collected it himself. In fact, I think I'll bring her here for a visit!'

'She'd be more than welcome,' smiled Kerry, as they walked back up to the yard.

Just as they arrived, Bea emerged from the cafe holding a big tray of cakes. Sammi's mum and their neighbour went up to give her some help, and began to hand them out on paper plates to anyone who wanted one.

'Oh, Bea! How fantastic! I thought we'd eaten all the cakes yesterday!' exclaimed Kerry.

'No, there was one tray left,' said Bea. 'And I've chopped them all in half so that more people can have a taste!'

Sammi's mum came back, pointing to the tray and then to the people who were gathering around hopefully.

'You want to hand out more cakes?' Bea asked her.

'More cakes,' repeated Sammi's mum, copying the words carefully. Then she laughed, and winked at Sammi. 'I learn quick!' she said.

Sammi laughed, and watched her waltz off with two more plates in her hands.

Giti ran up to Sammi and took his hand. 'Show me your friend,' she said to him in English. 'Your donkey friend.'

Just then, Sammi heard a distant sound from the behind the barn.

'Eeee-yore! Eeee-yore!' called Dusty.

How could he forget? 'Of course! I haven't told him the good news yet!' said Sammi. He pulled Giti towards the paddocks, and they broke into a run. 'Come on, Giti. Let's go and tell him right now!'

Epilogue

Sammi led Dusty into his stall and tied him up, then undid his saddle. He lifted it off and carried it up to the storeroom, whistling a tune.

'You sound cheerful!' commented Rory. He was up a ladder, repairing one of the old windows. Since City Farm had been given a new lease of life, Rory hadn't stopped sprucing it up – he'd painted fences and built new hutches and even started work on a whole new stall.

'I am always cheerful these days!' laughed Sammi.

He laid the saddle carefully on its rack, then returned to Dusty's stall and gave him a good brush down. 'You work hard today, Dusty.' he commented. 'I bet you looking forward to a good roll in the grass.'

Dusty had given about fifteen donkey rides to

younger children over the morning and lunch time, trotting up and down the main yard. Sammi had led him the whole time, and Dusty hadn't started braying once! He fed him a nice juicy carrot as a reward, then untied him and led him back out to the paddock. Dusty's ears were pricked as he walked through the gate, and Stanley whinnied a greeting.

'Now you go and enjoy yourself!' said Sammi. He slipped off Dusty's head collar and gave his neck a final pat.

Dusty butted Sammi's arm affectionately, then trotted off, braying noisily. Stanley stood still for a moment, then turned around and cantered wildly to the far end of the paddock with his tail held high. Dusty charged after him, and the two of them kicked their heels, just for the fun of it!

Sammi grinned, then jogged back to the barn. He'd better hurry up or he'd be late. He collected his kit bag and his football. It was Saturday afternoon, and all the boys would be waiting for him down the park.

He was just about to dash off to catch the bus when he remembered who was visiting City Farm today. He went to the cafe and popped his head around the door.

'Hi, Mum! Hi, Giti!' he called.

'Hello! Go play football! You late!' laughed his mum.

She was sitting with Bea, Giti and their neighbour, eating cake. 'What you still do here?'

'You want chocolate cake? It's very nice. Yummy,' said Giti, who had it smeared all around her mouth.

'It's OK, Giti,' Sammi told her. 'I don't want to eat cake before football – I like more to have it afterwards.'

'I'll save you some,' promised Giti.

'Don't believe a word,' said Bea. 'She'll eat it all herself!'

As the big old door closed behind him, Sammi remembered how he'd felt when he first saw the farm and the rickety barn. So much had changed since then. The Harvest Hope project had shown him that his new life wasn't so bad, after all. He had a whole new home, and City Farm was definitely part of it! Sammi gave them a final wave.

'Good luck! Come home safe!' called his mum, slipping back into Pashtun.

'Say it in English!' replied Sammi, over his shoulder.

'No problem,' said his mum. 'See you later, alligator!'

Sammi laughed. 'In a while, crocodile!'

CHARACTER PROFILE

ANIMAL: Donkey
ANIMAL NAME: Dusty

LIKES:

Making lots of noise and being with his friends.

DISLIKES:

Being quiet.

FAVOURITE PLACE:

A shady spot in the field.

FAVOURITE FOOD:

Carrots.

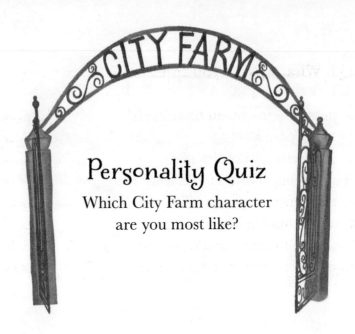

Personality Quiz

Which City Farm character
are you most like?

Q1. What's your favourite type of animal?

a) goats	0 points
b) dogs	2 points
c) cats	4 points
d) pigs	6 points
e) horses	8 points
f) ducks	10 point
g) donkeys	12 points
h) you don't mind, you like them all!	14 points

Q2. What upsets you most?

a) people being mean to animals   12 points
b) being poorly   4 points
c) your parents not listening   2 points
d) not being allowed to do what you want   8 points
e) teachers telling you off   0 points
f) your family being poorly   10 points
g) people thinking you're stupid   6 points
h) not being able to understand   12 points

Q3. Would you rather...

a) eat cakes in the café   10 points
b) play football   12 points
c) draw or paint   0 points
d) play with the animals   14 points
e) do something active   8 points
f) listen to music   4 points
g) read a book   2 points
h) work on the farm   6 points

Turn over to see who you are...

Personality Quiz

0-4 points: You are Darren. You're creative and artistic, and you can be a bit of a rebel. Your perfect pet is one that can be a bit naughty, just like Basher the goat!

4–8 points: You are Emily. You're sensitive and a bit shy. You can get a bit lonely at times, so make sure you spend lots of time with your friends, and loving animals like Patch the dog!

8–12 points: You are Laura. You're sweet and funny and animals love you! You can overcome any obstacle that you set your mind to.

12-18 points: You are Jack. You are patient and clever. You love working outdoors and don't mind getting your hands dirty.

18-24 points: You are Zoe. You are very determined and you love having a hobby. Make sure you remember to relax sometimes!

24-30 points: You are Katie. You like being at home and you love your family. People enjoy spending time with you because you're so kind.

30-36 points: You are Sammi. You are very loyal and lots of fun. It can take a while to get to know you, but the friends you have are friends for life – just like Dusty the donkey!

36-42 points: You are Asha. You are energetic and fun and you love animals more than anything.

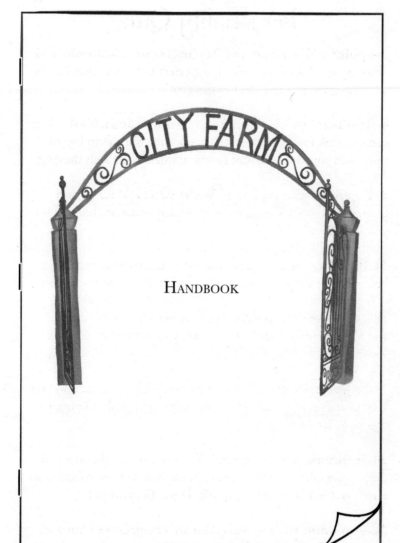

HANDBOOK

CITY FARM RULES:

Lots of people visit City Farm everyday. Follow these simple rules to make sure that everyone enjoys themselves.

- Treat people – and animals – with respect and kindness.

- Help out and join in! If you can see someone needs a hand, offer to help them.

- Don't feed the animals, some of them are on special diets, and different food will upset their tummies.

- Wash your hands! Most of the City Farm animals like to be held and stroked, but you should always wash your hands afterwards.

- Have fun!

Our Guinea Pigs:

Bubble and Squeak are our guinea pigs. They're very friendly and love being held and petted every day.

🐾 Guinea pigs originally come from South America and usually live until they are five or six years old.

🐾 Guinea pigs are very social creatures and Bubble and Squeak would get very lonely if they didn't have each other. They like having lots of hay and straw to burrow in, and toilet-roll tubes to use as tunnels.

🐾 Guinea pigs are active up to 20 hours per day and sleep only for short periods.

🐾 Guinea pigs make lots of different noises which mean different things. When they're excited they make lots of squeaking 'wheek' sounds and they purr when they're being stroked.

Our Equines:

*City Farm is lucky enough to have a pony called Stanley,
an ex-racehorse called Swift and a donkey called Dusty. Horses
and donkeys take a lot of looking after.*

🐎 Our horses and donkeys need to be mucked out every morning, and given a pile of fresh straw for their beds.

🐎 They have small feeds at breakfast and lunchtime, and each have a net full of hay in the evening. During the day they are 'turned out' into the field for at least six hours so that they can graze on the grass.

🐎 We always check that there are no holes in the fencing, and no broken glass or poisonous plants before they are turned out into the paddock.

🐎 In the winter, Dusty, Stanley and Swift have stable rugs on their backs so they don't get cold.

Our Pig:

Cynthia is City Farm's Tamworth pig. She loves playing football!

♘ Pigs are actually very clean. When Cynthia rolls in the mud it's because she's hot. Pigs can't sweat, so they cover themselves in cool mud, which cools them down and protects their skin from the sun.

♘ Pigs are also very smart, and they learn tricks faster than dogs. They like to have toys like a football to keep them entertained.

♘ Tamworth pigs are a gingery-orange colour, and they originally come from the UK.

♘ Pigs have such a good sense of smell that they can find things buried underground.

♘ It is actually illegal to give pigs scraps from the kitchen.

Our Goats:

City Farm has five goats – dairy goats Nelly and Nancy, male goats Billy and Bramble, and a new goat, naughty little Basher.

◖ Dairy goats need milking every day. More people in the world drink goats' milk than cows' milk. Goat's milk makes delicious cheeses.

◖ Goats can live between 12 and 16 years.

◖ Goats only have teeth on their bottom jaw, the top is a hard palate.

◖ Goats are often very good at escaping their pens – like Basher – so we have to make sure their enclosures are secure.

◖ Baby goats are called kids, and goats can have up to six kids per litter.

Our Chickens and Ducks:

*There are lots of chickens and ducks at City Farm, and more
ducklings and chicks hatch every year.*

- Chickens and ducks need a shed to sleep in at night,
  otherwise they might get eaten by foxes.

- Very few ducks actually "quack", but ducks do make
  a wide range of noises.

- Ducks have webbed feet that act like paddles, and
  their feathers are waterproof.

- Chickens preen their feathers every day, and like to
  take dust baths in the farmyard.

Our Sheep:

Curly and Lizzie are City Farm's Greyface Dartmoor Sheep.
They have floppy fringes that fall over their eyes and are very
woolly and cuddly!

Female sheep are called ewes, male sheep are called rams, and baby sheep are called lambs.

Sheep like to live together in a flock. If one moves, the others will follow. When people copy what each other do without thinking, it's called being a sheep.

Sheep have to be shorn every year, and their wool is spun into thread that makes clothes, blankets, and lots of other things.

Sheep were some of the first animals to be domesticated by people.

7

Our *City Farm* and the *Harvest Hope* project
are fictional, but there are real city farms
all around the country and they often
need volunteers. Why not go and visit the
one nearest to you?

For more exciting books from brilliant
authors, follow the fox!
www.curious-fox.com